John Rowe Townsend was born in Leeds and educated at Leeds Grammar School and Cambridge University where he read English. After working as a journalist on the *Yorkshire Post* and the *Evening Standard*, he joined the *Guardian* where he was editor of the weekly international edition and reviewer of children's books.

He began writing full-time in 1969, but continues to do some reviewing and lecturing.

Books by the same author

Cloudy-Bright

Dan Alone

Downstream

A Foreign Affair

Forest of the Night

Good-Night, Prof, Love

Good-bye to Gumble's Yard
(Originally *Widdershins Crescent*)

Gumble's Yard

Hell's Edge

The Intruder

The Islanders

Noah's Castle

The Persuading Stick

Pirate's Island

Rob's Place

The Summer People

Tom Tiddler's Ground

Top of the World

The Xanadu Manuscript

Modern Poetry
A Sounding of Storytellers
Written for Children

JOHN ROWE TOWNSEND

King Creature Come

Richard Drew Publishing
Glasgow

First published by
Oxford University Press 1980

This edition first published 1988 by

Richard Drew Publishing Limited
6 Clairmont Gardens, Glasgow G3 7LW
Scotland

The publisher acknowledges the financial assistance of the
Scottish Arts Council in the publication of this book.

British Library Cataloguing in Publication Data

Townsend, John Rowe, *1922*—
    King Creature come.
    I. Title
    823'.914[J]

    ISBN 0-86267-221-X

Printed and bound in Great Britain by
Cox & Wyman Ltd., Reading

Chapter One

You could say it all began with the arrival of the relief ship. Or you could say it started two or three years before that, with the disappearance of Harmony's sister, Melody. But I think myself it began the day I saw the Creature prowling around the garbage. And that sight probably wouldn't have made the impression it did if I hadn't just been talking to Harmony on the subject of the Creatures.

We were sitting in a corner of the big lounge in the Central Tower, and as usual everyone was playing the Dimension Game. Everyone, that is, except us. I didn't want to play the Game because I played it so badly. Harmony didn't want to play, either. She always said she was bored with the Game, though we knew she could play it well enough if she chose. Older Persons told her she would grow out of this attitude.

The servant, a female Creature of nondescript appearance, had just brought her something to drink. Harmony smiled at it and said, 'Thank you very much.' And the Creature, more embarrassed than pleased, mumbled something under its breath and backed away.

I looked at Harmony with an expression of mild surprise. She laughed.

'Don't you like me to speak to a Creature?' she asked.

'I couldn't see that there was any need for it.'

'No,' she said. 'The serving Creatures aren't really there, are they, so far as most of us are concerned? One just looks through them, without even noticing them.'

'Well, you *don't* notice them, unless you make a point of it,' I said. 'At least, *I* don't. They don't *want* to be noticed.'

'Not that it matters much what Creatures want,' Harmony remarked.

'Well, no, of course not,' I said. 'They *are* only Creatures, after all.'

She leaned towards me, close enough for the golden cloud surrounding her head to touch my cheek.

'Vector,' she asked, 'doesn't it ever occur to you that the Creatures are very much like us?'

I was startled. I knew already that Harmony was apt to have wild ideas. But this was going rather far.

'I've heard it before,' I said, trying to keep the surprise out of my voice. 'But I must admit I can't see it myself.'

At that she sounded impatient. 'You don't *want* to see it!' she declared. 'No Person ever wants to see it.'

'But you only have to use your eyes,' I objected. 'You can see at a glance how different they are.'

'You can see at a glance how similar they are!' she retorted. 'They have heads, haven't they, and eyes and noses and ears? And they move around and eat and drink.'

'You could say that of animals,' I reminded her, 'and nobody says that animals are the same as us.'

'Creatures can talk, too,' she said.

'Well, yes, after a fashion. But only in a primitive way. You couldn't have a real conversation with a Creature. Even Helix would hardly claim that!'

And at the mention of Helix a thought occurred to me. 'You've been talking to him out of class!' I said.

'Perhaps I have,' she admitted.

Helix was tutor to both of us, and to the other four young Persons of the Colony. His job was to give us a proper Personic education in music, mathematics and the Game, and in class he stuck to it conscientiously. But it was said that in out-of-class discussion he would come up with far-fetched theories about the Creatures, on the history and biology of which he was a great expert.

There wasn't, of course, much competition to be an expert on the Creatures. Helix's interest was shared only by old Cosine, the former Regent, who had the bizarre conviction that in the distant past Creatures had actually composed music; and Cosine was generally held to be a little off balance.

Myself, I rather liked Helix. But I didn't take his views on the Creatures seriously, and I was sure that even he couldn't deny the impossibility of exchanging ideas with a Creature. The Creatures had their language, of course, but it was a primitive instrument, suitable mainly for dealing with everyday objects and occurrences. Our philosophy, our music and mathematics, our whole ways of thought were far outside its range. How, for instance, could one explain the Dimension Game in words that would mean anything to these beings who couldn't even grasp elementary relativity, and whose idea of an intellectual contest was the childish affair they called chess? Even our names – musical for females, mathematical for males – were untranslatable into Creature, though for the purpose of the present account I have tried to find rough equivalents.

And yet ... if you set your mind to overcoming its natural resistance to any such idea, you could see that there was in fact a resemblance between Persons and Creatures. In some ways the Creatures were like coarse copies of ourselves. Their heads were rounder than ours, their foreheads lower. The eyes were very much like our own, but with coloured irises, mainly in variations of brown and blue. Skin tones ranged from a pale, pinkish fawn through yellows and browns to near-black. According to Helix, these differences resulted from genetic adjustment to climate in times when a far larger part of the land surface of this planet had been inhabited. They did not appear to have any significance now.

The oddest feature of the Creatures, and one which I remember had half-fascinated and half-horrified me when I first arrived on Earth, was that in place of the clouds of fine spun gold surrounding our own heads, they had patches of thick, straight or curly hair which clung closely to their scalps. This hair varied in shade, having some relationship to skin colour; but if a Creature lived long enough its hair would turn white. Sometimes the hair would disappear as the Creature aged. Patches of hair also occurred in a few other places on the Creatures' bodies; adult males had them on the chin and upper lip.

This coarse hairiness had always seemed to me to make it clear

3

that Creatures were not really human, as did the small, useless claws they had on the ends of their fingers and toes. They were squat, the tops of their heads coming a little above our shoulders. Their movements were clumsy, compared with ours. Even in favourable conditions, when employed as Guards or servants, or when strong and healthy enough to seize more than their share of the available food, Creatures had less than half our life-span. A Guard or domestic Creature was generally reckoned to have outlived its usefulness at sixty or seventy Earth years of age. Creatures whose whole lives were led outside the walls had even briefer lifespans: thirty or forty years, perhaps, on average, if they survived infancy.

As if to make up for their short life-span, the Creatures bred with ease and rapidity. It was perfectly possible for females to bear offspring every year, and it was not unknown for two or more births to take place at a time. This high rate of breeding was taken by us to be another indication that the Creatures were of a different and inferior order; though Helix had been known to say that we could do with some of it ourselves.

Actually, of course, we saw little of the Creatures in their wild state. The only ones with whom we had any regular contact were the servants and Guards; and the Guards in particular were so highly trained as hardly to seem like Creatures at all. They wore a standard dress known as uniform, which was based on some almost-forgotten Earth tradition and signified that they held a position of minor authority. They were able to drive and maintain our craft and use our communicating equipment; indeed, these duties were almost entirely delegated to them. They kept the lesser Creatures in order, and from their earliest years they were trained in our service. We trusted the Guards.

And Harmony, reacting to my remark about the difficulty of holding conversation with Creatures, reminded me at once about Node, who until recently had been Tower Guard in the block where she and I and the other young Persons lived.

'We used to talk to Node,' she said now. 'And tease him a bit, I'm afraid.'

'Yes, *but*,' I said impatiently, 'that wasn't real talk, with friends, about ideas.'

4

'Not about ideas, maybe. Guards are practical. But I always looked on Node as a friend. He was cheerful and very patient with us. I must go and see how he likes his new job.'

'Are you getting out of balance, Harmony, or am I? I don't understand you. Node was a perfectly good Tower Guard, and if there was something wrong with the air- or light-conditioning you could tell him about it and he'd get it fixed, but as for being a *friend*. . . . A Guard is only a Creature, when all's said and done, and you couldn't call a Creature a friend.'

'You know, Vector,' Harmony said, 'there are times when I despair of you. In fact when I hear you being so obstinate I could almost hate you!'

'*Hate* me!' I repeated, shocked. 'You don't have to be foul-mouthed. Hate isn't Personlike.'

'Personlike! If I hear that word once more, I really think I *shall* go off balance!'

I felt myself growing indignant. In another minute I might have said something unPersonlike myself. Perhaps it was just as well that at that moment Cadenza and the three boys came up and asked Harmony to join them at the composing-board. Harmony had no patience with the Game, but music was another matter. She threw me a last, impatient look, then shrugged her shoulders and went off with them. I decided she didn't like me any more than I liked her. And, feeling depressed and disgruntled, I wandered from the lounge, descended the climb, and went for a walk in the Precinct.

The Precinct was the area outside the Towers but inside the Colony walls. It was safely covered in from Earth weather, and the light and air were as fully controlled as in the Towers themselves. There was no tiresome view of the teeming, Creature-filled city outside. In the Precinct were light-fountains and sculpture to please and soothe the eye; there were small lawns and flower-beds, and seats were provided in case anyone should wish to sit there for individual thinking. The seats were not much used, though; for in spite of being enclosed, the Precinct had about it a slight suggestion of open air which made many Persons uneasy.

I don't suppose I'd have gone anywhere near the guardroom if it hadn't been for Harmony's remarks about Node. Though she had irritated me, her words had had some effect. It was absurd to speak of Node as a friend, but he'd always appeared to be devoted to us when he worked in our Tower. I hadn't spoken to him since his promotion to Guardroom Commander. It would be good to hear how he was getting on. And there was no one else to talk to; all the Persons I knew were engaged in the usual Personlike pursuits.

The guardroom was close to the big main gate, which stood open today because the early-autumn Earth weather was mild, and with a little de-oxygenation the air was quite comfortable for Persons. Next to the main gate was a door used by Guards and licensed Creatures. Outside it in the early morning Creatures would line up for any work that might be available; and later they would line up again at a side window for their day's pay. Between guardroom and main gate lay a small courtyard, into which supplies rolled daily from the farms and gardens in the hills, and from which garbage went out each morning on a couple of cumbersome, old-fashioned land-craft.

Node sprang up when I went into the guardroom, and stood stiffly with his feet together, putting his hand to the side of his head in the curious gesture known as saluting. He was a round-faced, thickset Creature whose greying hair had a tendency to curl. He wore the usual Guard uniform, with a badge to show his seniority, and like all Guards he had shaved the lower parts of his head. I would have found it hard to know him by his face only, because all Creatures looked much alike to me; but his broad grin, cheerful manner and ready speech – bordering on the familiar, Cadenza used to say – distinguished him from other Guards I knew, who tended to be sullen and silent.

'Sir?' he said now, in an inquiring tone. Guards were not supposed to begin conversations with Persons; they were expected to await their orders.

'How do you like the new life, Node?' I asked him.

'Oh, not so bad, sir. Missing you all, if I may say so. And Miss Harmony in particular.'

'Speak freely, Node,' I told him. And Node began telling me about guardroom hours and duties, and how they differed from those of the servants. I listened patiently, feeling a little bored and looking now at him, now out through the window into the courtyard.

'Course, sir, servants is hardly better than ordinary Creatures,' he was remarking in tones of scorn, when I noticed movement among the cluster of garbage bins that stood in a corner of the yard awaiting collection. One of the lids was gradually rising, a centimetre or two at a time. It took me a few seconds to realize that there was something concealed behind the row of bins and stealthily raising that lid. I watched but didn't say anything while I half-listened to Node. And after a few more seconds I saw a thin, ragged Creature slipping cautiously from one bin to the next in the direction of the gate. Clutched to its skinny chest it had a mess of what looked like old fruit and vegetable remnants.

And then I saw that I was not alone in observing it. One of Node's under-Guards, standing on the guardroom steps, was watching it intently, while another moved towards the gate to cut off its retreat.

'You, there!' the first Guard roared; and the Creature stood up, dropping its unappetizing load. The Guard hurled a lump of something at it, narrowly missing, and the Creature ran for the gate. It saw that its way was blocked, and doubled back round the bins. And then a third Guard came into sight, and the Creature was trapped. They caught it just below the guardroom window, no more than a metre from my face.

Node had joined me at the window.

'Well, they got that one!' he said, laughing heartily. He pushed the window open.

'Go easy, lads,' he told them. 'Give it enough to teach it a lesson, that's all!' And then, to me,

'Look away, sir, if you don't like it. Rough and ready, that's us, but our instructions is to show them they can't steal and get away with it.'

'It was only garbage,' I said.

'Maybe, sir, but if we let them take garbage today, there's no telling what they'll be after tomorrow. They have to learn to keep their thieving hands to themselves.' He paused, then added, 'It's a kindness to them really, if they did but know it.'

Any other time I should probably have looked away. It wasn't any concern of Persons to examine the way the Guards did their job. They got their rations, their uniform, their small privileges

7

and their power over the common Creatures; and so long as they saw that we weren't bothered with the tiresome details of daily management I knew we weren't supposed to interfere. But Harmony's remarks of half an hour ago were still echoing in my mind, and I watched the little scene with some interest. If this was how Guards treated a Creature after being exhorted to go easy, I wouldn't have liked to see them in a less restrained mood.

The three subordinate Guards were now pushing the Creature to and fro between them, so that it staggered at each thrust and almost fell. It was a wretched specimen, lank and filthy, with greyish-white face and tangled hair. At each shove the Guards laughed. I wondered how long they could keep it up. At last one of them seemed to tire, and instead of sending the Creature flying again he held it upright by its narrow shoulders.

'You know what happens to things like you?' he asked it; and without warning he hit it in the mouth. Its head jerked, and a thin trickle of blood came from its mouth corner.

Then the Creature looked in my direction. And suddenly, in its wild, frightened eyes, I became aware of a desperate intensity of appeal; there was a transmission of naked feeling from the Creature to myself that I didn't know how to cope with. In all my four years in the Colony I'd never experienced such emotional shock. It must have thrown me instantly out of balance. I couldn't prevent myself from doing what I did next. Defying all reason and propriety I thrust my head through the open window and shouted,

'Stop it! Stop it, I say. At once!'

The effect was instantaneous. The three Guards dropped their hands to their sides and stood stock-still, facing the window. The Creature pulled itself together and dashed for the gate. In seconds it had vanished, leaving nothing behind but the small pathetic mess of squashed fruit and vegetables. Node stepped forward.

'All right, lads,' he said to the Guards. 'Don't chase it. To your posts. Dismiss!'

Then he turned to me.

'You shouldn't have done that, sir,' he said chidingly.

'I didn't like the way they were treating that Creature.'

'You didn't have to watch,' Node said. And then his tone changed and became familiar.

'Listen here, young Vector,' he said. 'You're on the verge of becoming a grown Person. I'm not your equal nor ever can be, but I've known you for years and cared about you. And I'm going to give you a bit of advice. It's this. You mind your own business!'

'Node!' I objected sharply. 'Even if you *have* known me for years, that's not the way to speak to a Person!'

Node grinned. 'There's only the two of us present,' he said. 'And considering the number of times I should have reported you for childish misbehaviour when I was a Tower Guard, I reckon you owe me a bit of tolerance. So I'm going to speak plain to you. I know what Persons are, I've dealt with them long enough. You're occupied with all them clever things that we don't understand. Well, we're occupied with things that you don't understand, likewise. Such as the nature of Creatures and what stops them getting out of hand. You pay us to protect you, and we do it. But you don't want to know what goes on down here, and it's better that you shouldn't. So if I was you, sir, I'd just keep right out of things that didn't concern me!'

'Such as what, Node?' a voice inquired.

Node and I both turned round. A Person had come quietly into the guardroom from the direction of the main gate. It was Helix, tutor to myself and the other young Persons. He was broad-shouldered and powerfully built, and he towered over Node. His voice was strong and firm. He was a formidable figure, and Node reacted instantly to him, putting the respect back into his voice.

Not that Node was disconcerted. 'I was just venturing, sir,' he said, 'to explain to young Mr Vector the procedures what we follow here, and to suggest that we could be trusted to perform our duties without being supervised.'

'Oh,' said Helix. He looked quizzically from Node to myself and back again. Node met his eyes with a blank stare.

'Your procedures wouldn't have anything to do with that wretched Creature that just shot out through the gate as if the dogs were after him?' Helix inquired.

'I know nothing about that, sir,' Node said.

My mouth opened, but I closed it again without saying anything. It was true that Node had kept silent on several past occasions when he could have got me into trouble. And Helix was one of the very few Persons who might have seen fit to make an issue of this small incident.

'I thought you noticed quite a lot, Node,' Helix remarked mildly. 'I thought, indeed, it was the job of a gate Guard to notice things.'

Node met his eye once more. I had the impression that he and Helix had had previous encounters and knew each other well.

'Oh, yes, sir,' Node said. 'We notice lots of things. Lots and lots of things!'

'Indeed!' said Helix. His tone was sharper now. 'Be careful, Node. And remember that Vector will soon be a full Person, and treat him accordingly.'

'Yes, sir,' Node said. 'My apologies, Mr Vector, if I spoke out of turn.' But there was nothing submissive in his voice, and as Helix and I went out of the guardroom I could have sworn that Node momentarily closed an eye in the signal of complicity that the Creatures called a wink.

'If you're not doing anything in particular, Vector,' said Helix, 'perhaps you could spare me a few minutes.' He led me past the sculpture and the light-fountains to the flower garden, and we sat on a bench together. Helix looked at me thoughtfully.

'Something happened then that disturbed you,' he said. 'I could see it in your face. You were quite shaken.'

I didn't say anything.

'And I suspect it was something to do with that Creature.'

I still stayed silent.

'There was blood on his face,' Helix went on. 'Fresh blood.'

I made no comment, but winced.

'They'd been beating him up, hadn't they?'

There was no point in holding out on him.

'Yes, they had,' I said. 'The Creature was stealing from the garbage bins. They shoved it around, and one of them hit it in the mouth.'

'It,' Helix said musingly. 'It. How would it feel to be referred to as "it"?'

'What?'

'Nothing. But Vector, it bothered you that the Creature was ill-treated. This interests me. It wouldn't bother every Person, you know.'

'According to Node,' I said, 'most of us don't know or want to know what goes on down here.'

'Node's quite right.'

'And he says it's better that we shouldn't.'

'That's a different proposition,' Helix said. He paused for a moment, then went on, 'And it's not just what goes on down here. It's what goes on out there.'

'You mean in the city, I suppose,' I said. 'But surely *that* doesn't concern us?'

Helix looked at me with a strange expression. 'It doesn't?' he said. And I hesitated, suddenly confused.

'We lead a very insulated life,' Helix remarked, after waiting a moment or two for a response. 'Music, mathematics, the Game....'

'It seems to satisfy most people,' I said.

'Perhaps so. Does it satisfy you?'

'I'm not really musical,' I said. 'And I'm terrible at the Game.'

'Yet you don't strike me as stupid.'

'Thank you,' I said drily.

'It's always a pity not to be musical,' Helix said. 'But to be bored with the Game might not necessarily be a bad thing.'

'I didn't say I was bored with the Game. I said I was terrible at it.'

'But you *are* bored with it, aren't you?'

'Yes.'

'That's why you're bad at it.... You interest me, Vector. I feel you may be on the verge of making all kinds of discoveries.'

There was silence again for a minute or two. Then, 'You needn't answer this if you don't want, Vector. But am I right if I guess that you're becoming a full male?'

I felt myself blushing. This was a shockingly unPersonlike question.

'I don't know why one should be embarrassed,' Helix said. 'All this is important to our future, after all.'

'But it's ... *physical*,' I protested.

Helix smiled.

'Spoken like a true Person,' he said.

'Anyway, I don't know whether I am or not,' I said. 'I haven't seen the doc.'

'You don't need to see the doc. If you are, you know you are. It's unmistakable.'

'All right,' I said unhappily. 'Yes, I am. And what of it? It's not exactly a privilege, is it?'

'I'm afraid not. With all the full women being sent Home to Annulus for childbearing, there's not much point in being male. You could volunteer for the operation, of course.'

'I don't fancy that.'

'You'd *have* to have it if you misbehaved yourself.'

'I know. But I still don't fancy it.'

'Good for you,' Helix said.

'You're ... a full male yourself, aren't you?' I inquired, still embarrassed.

'Yes. And it can be frustrating. Especially as I don't believe it's really necessary to send the women Home. I'm convinced they could bear children successfully here on Earth.'

I stared.

'But that's never happened,' I said.

'It's never been allowed to happen.' Then, after a pause, 'At least, hardly ever.'

I looked at him inquiringly. I saw that for once Helix himself was embarrassed. And a bit of old gossip floated into my mind. Normally I'd have kept quiet about it, but this seemed to be a day for saying outrageous things. So I said one.

'Didn't I once hear that you were born in the Colony?' I asked.

Helix had recovered by now.

'Quite right,' he said. 'So far as I know, I'm the only Person who ever was. My mother didn't look like a full woman and never told anybody she was one, so they didn't send her Home when she reached childbearing age. And, yes, I was born here.'

'Who ever would have *dared* ...?' I said, half marvelling, half horrified.

'That's one thing I'm not going to tell you.'

'If they'd send the full men Home, too, it wouldn't be so bad,' I said. I had always wished I had some chance of seeing our own world, Annulus, again. We knew so much about it, and talked about it so much. I was sure it would be vastly more exciting than this little colony on an unimportant planet so many light years away. But I knew very well there was no hope.

'No room on the ships,' Helix said, putting my knowledge into words. 'And it's women they need, not men. We're much less essential. So it's the Colony for us, and the operation if we want it. Still, I'm glad you don't want it, Vector. Persons are tame enough already, don't you think?'

'We're supposed to be civilized,' I said. 'Not wild.'

Helix smiled.

'This colony,' he said, 'is a triumph of civilization, or so its members think. But when Persons know and care so little about what happens outside, and when a decent Guard like Node can tolerate the brutality you've just seen, I begin to wonder.... Vector, have you ever been outside the walls?'

'Yes,' I said. 'I've been to the Summer Valley four or five times, on vacation.'

'Oh, of course. But that's only changing one precinct for another. You flew high, I suppose?'

'I don't really know. It was a windowless craft. We couldn't see anything.'

'Didn't you *want* to see anything?'

'Most people just wanted not to be sick.'

'And apart from that you've never been outside?'

'I haven't *needed* to, Helix,' I said patiently. 'Why should I want to go outside? What is there to go outside *for*?'

Helix sighed. 'To think,' he said, 'that I've been in charge of your education for four years, and after all that time you have so little curiosity about the world beyond the Precinct.'

'But you're only supposed to teach us music, mathematics and the Game. That's what education's about, isn't it?'

'So it would appear. I mustn't tell you things that might trouble your tender minds. And Cadenza and the boys would soon complain if I did. But once you've reached Personhood I shan't have to be protective any longer. I'm looking forward to that. I hope you won't all feel you know everything you want to know, and stop seeing me.'

I didn't understand what he was getting at. It sounded rather disconcerting. My mind had been troubled by the guardroom incident, and I wasn't anxious to have it troubled still more by Helix.

'In the meantime,' Helix went on thoughtfully, 'I could at least find some excuse for getting you out of here for an hour or two. Why don't I take the group to the Survey Station next week?'

'It's twenty kilometres away,' I pointed out.

'That's not far in a craft. We'll take one of those small open ones.'

'A small open craft!' I wasn't at all sure I wanted a trip on a small open craft. I seemed to remember hearing of a craft two or three years before that had had propulsion failure and come down in the city. Its six occupants had had to find their way on foot to the Precinct, through Creature areas. They'd made it without incident, but still, there was no telling what might have happened.

'I don't know whether I fancy it,' I said.

'Come, now, don't be tame *and* timid,' Helix exhorted me. 'There's hope for you, Vector, and that might mean hope for others. You don't know what I mean? Well, never mind now. I'm going to propose a trip to the Survey Station, and I rather think Cadenza and the boys will decline with thanks. But I expect *you* to go.'

'Juniors aren't supposed to go outside,' I objected.

'You can go for an educational purpose, with me in charge. And there's another Person I expect to go. Harmony. You'd like to go on a trip with Harmony, wouldn't you?'

'I don't mind. She might not want to go on a trip with *me*. Harmony's not interested in me.'

'No? She might be more interested than you suppose. And she might be more interested still if she thought you had a sense of adventure, and some ideas beyond the two Ms and the Game. You could find new horizons, Vector, in more ways than one.'

He got up, slapped me jovially on the back in a gesture more characteristic of Node than of a Person, and walked away.

'Think about it, Vector!' he said over his shoulder. 'Just think about it!'

14

Chapter Two

Helix had been quite right about Cadenza and the three boys. They all groaned when he mentioned a visit to the Survey Station.

'Do we *have* to do that?' Secant asked wearily.

'What is there at the Survey Station anyway?' Median demanded. 'It was abandoned years ago, wasn't it?'

'Not totally abandoned,' Helix said. 'There's still a handful of Guards taking care of the premises and the equipment. You'd find it quite interesting to look around. And it would be a trip outside. A change for you.'

But this suggestion only brought more groans.

'You'd rather stay here and play the Game?' Helix asked.

There was a chorus of 'Yes' from all four of them.

'We're not nearly good enough at the Game,' Secant said. 'We're supposed to graduate at the end of this year.'

'I expect you'll manage it,' Helix said. 'And if you didn't, would it really matter?'

Secant drew breath sharply. Cadenza said,

'No, Helix dear, it wouldn't matter – except that we'd be officially children for another year, and we've been children long enough. We want to join the adults now.'

'And we've none of us mastered Manœuvre 14,' Centroid added.

'Even after all these years,' Helix said, 'it seems extraordinary to me that adult status should depend on proficiency in the Dimension Game.'

'It's vocational, isn't it?' Median said. 'It fits us to take our place in society. What's wrong with that?'

He sounded faintly aggrieved, but the others smiled.

'Dear Helix,' said Cadenza indulgently. 'We shall miss your

sessions when we graduate. But Median's right, isn't he? We do need to get on with what really matters.'

'And that's what really matters, isn't it?' Helix said. If I hadn't been talking to him in the Precinct a couple of days before, I might have missed the faintly ironic note in his voice.

'Well, listen,' he went on, 'why don't you four stay behind and practise Manœuvre 14 among yourselves? I'll discuss your difficulties with you later. And in the meantime I'll take Harmony and Vector to the Survey Station.'

That delighted them. Cadenza touched Helix's hand in the adult gesture of affection.

'Just what we need,' she said. 'Enjoy yourselves.' And without giving Helix a chance to change his mind they promptly disappeared towards the Game Lounge, where most of the adult colonists were already at play.

'You see?' Helix said. 'They really *are* almost adults. And they may as well graduate and devote themselves to the Game. They'll never do anything else, I'm afraid. But I do try, don't I?'

'I thought you were trying a little too hard,' Harmony said. 'What if they'd decided to come after all?'

'Then I might have had six promising students instead of two,' said Helix.

'I don't think so, somehow,' Harmony said. And she smiled at me in a friendly way. I was surprised. I hadn't spoken to Harmony since she had been so impatient with me the other day. I wondered if Helix had said anything to her about the incident with the Creature and our conversation afterwards. I thought it probable that he had.

Actually I was feeling apprehensive at the thought of going outside the air-conditioned, light-controlled safety of the Colony, to say nothing of flying in an open craft. Like all Persons, I'd had it impressed upon me since early childhood that life was precious and one had no right to risk one's own. But I tried to put a brave face on it, and if Helix and Harmony noticed my nervousness they didn't say anything.

Helix took us up the climb and out on to the roof of the big Central Tower. Before going through the airlock Harmony and I took goggles and breathers from the dispenser. Helix ignored them

16

both, strode across the roof, and pressed the button for a craft.

'No breather, Helix?' Harmony asked. 'No goggles?'

'I don't use them,' Helix answered. 'I soon get used to the light and air out here. But you'd better wear yours, I suppose. Observe the safety code.'

Even wearing breather and goggles I felt perilously exposed. The sky was clear, the sun bright, and a little breeze came across the flat roof. One's step seemed, willy-nilly, bouncier than in the Precinct.

Harmony was taking her breather off. She breathed deeply two or three times without apparent discomfort, then, to my relief, she put the breather on again.

'It's not unlike home air really,' Helix said. 'After all, this planet was chosen for its atmosphere. A bit more oxygen, a bit less pressure, that's all the difference there is. You'd survive in it perfectly well if you had to.'

The craft was slow to arrive. But eventually one of the hangar doors opened and it emerged and glided towards us. It was a shabby-looking affair. At the tiller was the squat figure of a Guard. I didn't know him, but I thought he wasn't as well turned out as he might have been. He stepped from the craft and made the usual hand-to-head gesture, rather sloppily.

'Your craft,' he said; and, after a pause, 'sir.'

'I hope that thing's safe,' Helix said, looking at the craft with some distaste. 'Seems a bit scruffy to me.'

'Staff shortage,' said the Guard promptly. 'No cleaners.'

'With all the Creatures there are who'd be glad of an hour or two's work,' said Helix, 'I wouldn't have thought that was much of an excuse.'

'We don't let Creatures get near the craft.'

'Anyway, is it properly maintained? That's the question.'

'It's maintained according to schedule,' the Guard said. His expression was sullen. 'It's safe, all right. I'm going on it myself, aren't I? I don't mean to break my own neck.'

'Actually,' said Helix, 'you're not going on it. I'll take the tiller myself.'

The Guard stared.

'Don't worry,' Helix added. 'I can drive a craft, you know. I

17

went out on them often, in days when the surveys were still active. We often drove our own.'

'As you please,' the Guard said. He shrugged his shoulders. 'Give me a release, that's all.'

He took his tablet from his pocket and Helix keyed in a release.

'I'm responsible for this vehicle now,' he said as we slid from the roof. 'I'll just see how she handles.' And he circled the Precinct while I gripped the handrail, feeling dizzy.

'A bit sluggish but otherwise all right,' Helix said. He levelled up and steered us away from the Colony. Harmony had now taken her goggles off and was blinking in the bright light. She shielded her eyes with her hand.

'Look, Vector, just look!' she cried. 'Oh, isn't this lovely? Look at the hills. And the river down there, with the sun shining on it. Take off your goggles, Vector! It won't hurt you!'

She turned towards me, smiling again, and touched my hand. Hesitantly, I plucked off the goggles. The light was indeed bright, but it wasn't actually painful. I blinked two or three times, shaded my eyes with my hand as Harmony was doing, and left the goggles off.

We were above the city, which spread itself over a broad, flat-bottomed valley at a point where two rivers joined. Behind us, a beacon of civilization, shone the cluster of towers we had just left: the Colony. Farther up the valley were the farmlands, and criss-crossing them the network of high perimeter fences which guarded the crops against marauding Creatures. Ahead of us were foothills, shading from green to blue; beyond them was the looming indigo of the mountains.

Harmony leaned over to me and quietly removed my breather. There was a slight breeze, stirred by the craft itself; the air seemed rich and almost intoxicating. A small white fluffy cloud moved across the sun; you could see its outline shadowed on the landscape if you looked down.

If you looked down. . . . I was still suffering from dizziness and apprehension; and yet it was an extraordinary experience to be outside, moving through the brilliant light and heady air. It was beautiful and terrifying all at once, as if a protective film had been peeled away from one's senses. Suddenly it was too much for me, and I shifted focus from the overwhelming sights around me to the deck of the craft itself. Helix stood at the tiller, smiling; Harmony leaned out over the rail, unaware for the moment of either of us, drinking in sense-impressions. For a few minutes there was silence among us, then Harmony asked,

'Where are you taking us, Helix?'

The craft, still above the city, was descending.

I looked down again, fighting my vertigo. The ground was nearer, much nearer. The city now stretched in all directions from where we were. There were the tangled alleyways, the tumbledown hovels in which the Creatures lived. And Helix was taking us lower still – perilously low, it seemed to me. We were so low that there were structures reaching as high into the air as we were, and careless navigation would have meant a collision.

'You know what those are?' Helix asked.

'The things that stick up here and there? Yes, of course I do. You can see them from the Towers. They're the Stumps. Creature stuff.'

'Yes, Creature stuff. Let's go in a bit nearer. I'd like you to have a look.'

We passed close to the top of one of the Stumps. Seen from this distance it was like a grimy, unsuccessful imitation of one of our Towers, built with blocks of some unidentifiable material of an off-white colour. It ended raggedly, a mere fifty metres or so above ground level, looking as if the top had been knocked off. There were oblong openings at intervals – obviously some kind of window system – and plants had rooted themselves here and there. From a distance you would have thought the structure was unoccupied, but when you came nearer you could see Creature faces, and one or two of them even came to the openings and peered out. A pigeon sat on a windowsill until a hand and arm shot out through the opening and grabbed it.

In front of the Stumps was an open space, and radiating from it were broad empty ways on which you could have taxied two or three craft abreast. You could see now that they divided the tangles of Creature dwellings into several neighbourhoods. A few Creatures had come out into these broad ways and were looking up at us, shading their eyes.

'A hundred thousand people live in this city,' Helix said.

'You mean Creatures?'

'He means people,' Harmony said. And an alarming thought struck me.

'How many of *us* are there?' I asked.

'It's just slipped below the three hundred. But I suppose there'll be a few dozen on the relief ship.'

'Then,' I said slowly, 'if you look on Creatures as people, you could say that most people are Creatures.'

'Brilliant,' said Harmony sardonically. 'If you try hard, you may yet be clever enough to play the Game. Or at least to play chess.'

I ignored the insult.

'They outnumber us,' I said. 'By about three hundred to one.'

'That's right.'

'It's a good job we have them under control,' I said.

'Actually we don't,' said Helix. 'Insofar as they're under control at all, the Guards do it for us. But the Guards don't really control them either; they just keep them out. Out of the Precinct, out of the farms, out of the Summer Valley. And while ever they keep on doing so, we're all right.'

'When you put it like that,' I said, 'it sounds precarious.'

'In my opinion,' said Helix, 'it *is* precarious. But the early settlers got it going, and it's lasted a hundred years. I suppose it could last quite a while yet.'

The craft circled even lower.

'We could land quite easily, couldn't we?' Helix said. 'And make a little excursion among the Creatures.'

'Oh, no! Suppose they rushed us!' I said. I looked anxiously at Harmony. But her expression was one of pain rather than alarm. Helix noticed it at once.

'I'm sorry,' he said. And suddenly it was not our tutor speaking but an awkward, embarrassed Person who might be one of us. 'I'd forgotten.'

'That's quite all right,' Harmony said in a small voice.

I must have looked puzzled, because she turned to me and said, deliberately but with obvious effort,

'We were thinking of Melody.'

'Melody?'

'My sister.'

'Oh, yes. Melody.' I was thoughtful. I could just recall Melody. She had been a little older than Harmony and had come out with us on the same ship.

'She used to talk of going among the Creatures,' Harmony said. 'And she disappeared. You don't remember, Vector?'

I remembered, with an effort. I hadn't thought about Melody for years. She was never mentioned.

'I suppose she's ...' Harmony hesitated. 'I suppose she's ... dead.'

I jumped at the indecent word. I knew what it meant, of course. Every Person knew what death meant. It meant the diminution by one of our community. And that was a threat, not only here in the tiny Earth Colony but also at Home. In the ancient past, it was said, Persons had been fertile – not with the rampant fertility of the Creatures, but fertile enough to replace themselves. And generation had succeeded generation, little if at all reduced. But few female Persons were fertile now, and fewer still were without adverse genes. Artificial reproduction had been disastrous; the gene bank was contaminated and we would never amass a clean one now. We had to rely on the increasingly reluctant ways of nature.

That was why young people were cherished, protected, urged not to place themselves at risk. That was why girls who might bear children were removed to the safety of Home and lived in dread that none of their babies might be viable. That was why everyone shied from the thought of death. Even now, long afterwards, I find it hard to put the word into this record. Death was the threat to us: not only of individual mortality but of doom for all. It was the ultimate obscenity; and here was Harmony using the word without warning in conversation.

Not that she was being casual about it. It was easy to see that she was distressed.

'She might not be dead,' Helix said. 'No one has ever seen a body.'

A body! A dead body! That was another indecency.

'Was she definitely known to have gone outside?' I asked when I'd recovered from this further shock.

'It's pretty certain,' Harmony said. 'They searched every corner

21

of all four Towers and every centimetre of the Precinct. And no trace was ever found.'

'Was there a craft missing?'

'No.'

'But there was a message, wasn't there?' Helix said.

'Yes. It was on her tablet. I saw it before it was erased. It said, "I can't stand it any more. I'm getting out."'

'You mean, out of the Colony?'

'Yes. I'm sure that's what she meant. She'd talked of it before, but no one had taken her seriously. I didn't really understand, I wasn't old enough. But I think she'd said she found the Colony suffocating.'

'So she was ... mad!' I exclaimed.

'She was a little odd,' Harmony admitted.

'A little! What would be real oddity, then?'

'Everyone thinks *I'm* odd,' said Helix.

'Odd, yes,' I said. 'But you're not out of your senses.'

'I believe,' Helix said slowly, 'that Melody was no odder than I am.'

'Then you *are* out of your senses!' I said. 'You mean to tell us a sane Person could turn her back on civilization and go out among the Creatures? The dirty, stinking, dangerous Creatures? She'd have had to be crazy!'

'I wouldn't be too sure of that,' Helix said.

'Anyway,' I went on, 'it's absolutely baffling. She couldn't have got over the walls, and you say there was no craft missing. So she'd have had to go out through the gate, past the guardroom. What about the gate Guards?'

'They wouldn't stop an adult Person going out,' Harmony said.

'Of course not. But they'd have remembered when inquiries came to be made.'

'It's possible that some Guard knew perfectly well what she was up to,' Helix said.

This was getting wilder and wilder.

'Listen, Harmony,' I said impatiently. 'All right, so your sister is crazy. She turns her back on civilized life. She decides to leave the Precinct of her own sweet will. The gate Guard doesn't notice her, or doesn't say anything. *Then* what does she do? What is there to do, outside the walls, all on your own, without human company? Nobody to talk to, nothing to eat. She must have known she couldn't survive outside.'

'There's water outside,' Harmony said. 'Plenty of water in the streams.'

'But no food.'

'What do you mean, no food?' Helix said. 'There's Creature food.'

'*Creature* food? She couldn't eat that!'

'Do you know what Creature food is?' Helix asked gently.

'No, I don't. I've never watched a Creature eat. I think I'd rather not.'

'*I* know,' Harmony said. 'But ... Vector's right, isn't he? Persons couldn't eat what Creatures eat.' She shuddered. 'The flesh of animals!'

I felt my gorge rise.

'The flesh of animals! They couldn't! Why, it's....' I had intended to say 'disgusting', but the word seemed totally inadequate. The idea was too horrible to believe.

'Is that really true, Helix?' I asked, when I had collected myself.

'Yes, they eat animal flesh,' Helix said coolly. 'When they can get it. For most of them, that isn't often. Creatures are hungry a good deal of the time.'

'Well, if that's their diet, I'm glad to hear they go hungry,' I said.

'They kill the animals first.'

'Does that make it any better?' I asked. Eating dead animals seemed hardly less revolting to me than eating them alive.

'They do have other food, don't they, Helix?' Harmony asked.

'Yes. They drink the milk of animals and eat the eggs of birds.'

'Ugh.'

'They eat fruit and vegetables, too. And cereals. Not very palatable kinds to us. But I'm sure they would sustain life.'

'Human life, you mean? Person life?'

'Yes. I'm positive that Melody could have survived. In fact I'm pretty certain she wouldn't have gone outside at all if she hadn't felt confident of surviving.'

'But why should she do it?' I demanded. 'Why, why, why?'

'She could have wanted to see the world.'

'You can see the world from a craft,' I said.

'She may have wanted to *experience* the world,' said Harmony.

'I think that's very likely,' Helix said.

'If she were my sister,' I said, 'I'd rather she ... ceased altogether than was degraded by living among the Creatures. You keep telling me they're almost human, but nobody else says so. You don't know what they might have done to her!'

'Vector!' said Helix angrily. 'That was uncalled-for.'

'I don't care what you think, Vector!' Harmony declared. 'She's my sister. Or was. I don't know which. But whatever she's done or whatever's been done to her, I know I'd rather she was alive than dead!'

Her voice rang strongly. Helix intervened before I could reply.

'I shouldn't be at all surprised if she were still alive,' he said. 'Not at all.'

'What makes you say that?' Harmony asked.

Helix put the tiller across in silence, changing the craft's course. We had left the Stumps well behind now. Two or three minutes went by, and he made no reply to Harmony. He seemed a little embarrassed, as if his last remark had been indiscreet. Harmony didn't press him, but after a while she said thoughtfully,

'There's a lot in your life that you don't tell anyone about, isn't there, Helix?'

'There's a lot in my life that I *can't* tell anyone about,' Helix said. And both were silent again.

'I'm sorry I said what I did, Harmony,' I told her.

'What? Oh, that? It doesn't matter, Vector.' She looked across at me, and I could see that there was hope in her eyes. Helix's hint, indiscreet or not, had cheered her. And obviously she bore me no malice. She stepped over, smiling, and touched my hand.

'Isn't this trip *glorious*?' she said.

This was the moment in which I knew something that I'd been afraid to face. The way I felt about Harmony. The feelings themselves were not new; they had been creeping up on me for some time but I'd been reluctant to acknowledge them. It was only the recognition that was sudden.

Harmony. I had known her, it seemed, for ever: in fact since we both arrived on the last relief ship, at the minimum age allowed for

Earth Colony. That was four years ago. We had studied together under Helix, alongside Cadenza and the three boys. We had sat in the junior lounge together through a couple of hundred of those weekly Family Hours, in which bored parents – who seemed no closer to us than any other adult Persons – sat trying to make conversation with their children, while longing to get back to their music or mathematics or (above all) the intricacies of the Game. We had teased the Creature nurses, outwitted the Tower Guards. We had been aware, I think, of some bond between us: perhaps a shared liking for Helix, odd as he was; perhaps a lack of interest in the Dimension Game; or possibly something different and much more elusive.

The realization came in this moment when she turned to me to share her delight in the movement of the craft through sunlit air. I noticed, too, as if it were for the first time, that her body was changing, had changed; that there was a new awareness in her posture, in the way she looked at me; that there was an aura about her which at that time I was conscious of but could not have described. I only knew there was a yearning in myself for physical contact.

Physical contact beyond a brief, light touch of hand on hand was of course unPersonlike in the extreme. Persons were fastidious in such matters. But the events of the last few days had sown in my mind the half-guilty yet vastly exciting thought that perhaps after all it was not the greatest of evils to be unPersonlike. What if one could indeed lead a more interesting, if more perilous life away from the Towers and the endless Dimension Game? The recognition that I was attracted to Harmony went with a wider, still more alarming yet exhilarating sense of liberation. I realized with a jolt that I'd shoved my goggles and breather into a pocket and forgotten about them.

Looking across at Helix, I saw at once that he knew already. As he stood at the tiller of the craft he was watching us with half an eye, and he'd interpreted my expression correctly.

'Yes, Vector,' he said. 'You and Harmony are not merely two Persons. You're a young man and a young woman.'

Harmony turned on him with sudden passion.

'What's the good of being a woman?' she demanded. 'You know

what happens to women. Packed off to Annulus for safe childbearing!'

'You don't want to go Home?' Helix inquired mildly.

'No, I do not! I want to stay and do things here. All kinds of things. You'd never guess!'

'I might,' said Helix.

'Listen,' I said. 'They can't send you Home until the relief ship comes. And it's weeks late already. It might never come.'

'I wish I thought it wouldn't!' said Harmony.

Chapter Three

Talking about Melody's disappearance, and experiencing a new range of feelings, had taken my mind off the perils of flight. I found I was now enjoying the trip. When Harmony asked Helix if she could take the tiller I was only momentarily startled. In fact I had an odd sensation in my fingers as if I'd like to be holding that tiller myself.

'It's all yours,' Helix said to Harmony, handing over. 'But we haven't far to go. Do you think you can land it?'

'It's not difficult, is it?'

'Not really. You just need a bit of common sense. Look, that's what we're heading for, the white building on the hill.'

We had crossed the city now, and scrubby land with only the occasional shack on it was rising beneath us. The hill we were approaching was an isolated foothill of the mountain range beyond. The building was at the top and had a small central dome; you could in fact see it from the Towers on clear days.

'Somebody's taken the masts down,' Helix said. 'Oh well, I suppose they were weather stuff, and since the meteorologists left they weren't serving any purpose.'

'When did they leave?' I asked. 'And why?'

'They went Home on the last relief ship. So did the geologists and other specialists. They were surveying all this area as a site for a much bigger colony. But that idea was dropped. We don't *need* a bigger colony.'

A new thought crossed my mind.

'Do we need this one?' I asked.

'Well, maybe not. I don't actually think we'll be taken off, though. Not worth the trouble. And we're just about self-supporting. They don't have to send us much.'

'Where shall I bring this thing down?' Harmony asked.

'There's plenty of room in front of the main door. The place does have a landing area, but we needn't use it. It's over there, behind the building. When the station was in use they had to provide for quite a number of craft at the same time.... That's odd! There are craft there now!'

'About a dozen of them,' said Harmony.

'*Very* odd. I wonder what they're doing here.'

'Are they part of the fleet?' I asked.

'Yes, of course. What else could they be? They're the fleet all right. And more than half of it, I'd say.'

'Who's in charge of the fleet?'

'A section of the Guards. They're under the control of the Head Guard, Dyne. I know him. Quite responsible, I'd have thought. He answers directly to the Regent.'

'How am I managing?' asked Harmony.

'Beautifully. Ease the stick up a bit. That's right. Now, in you go.... Steady!'

The craft bounced a couple of times on its rollers, then stood still on the lawn in front of the main door.

'Well done,' said Helix. I felt curiously jealous.

'I'm sure I could do it, too,' I said.

'Probably,' said Helix. 'Now, let's see if we can find out what's happening.'

The main door was closed. It was a stout, smooth, old-fashioned, Creature-proof door of some opaque metal. We got out of the craft. Helix took out his tablet and keyed a combination, but nothing happened. He frowned and keyed again, but the door still didn't move. There was no knob or handle such as one might well have expected to find on an old door like this. Helix rapped on it with his knuckles, but this made hardly a sound and there was no response. Then he kicked it, hard and repeatedly, making a good deal of noise.

'Puzzling,' he said. 'All those craft, a locked door that won't budge, and no response.'

'Was there really anything very interesting to see here?' I asked.

'Probably not. But that's not the point. Something's going on, and I'm mystified.'

28

'We can report it back at the Precinct,' Harmony said.

'Yes, I suppose that's what we'll have to do. There'll be an explanation, of course. But I feel frustrated, after bringing you all this way. I wish....'

And then the door slid back. A uniformed Guard stood in the opening. Unwinking and unbudging, with feet planted apart, he stared at us.

'Aren't you going to let us in?' Helix asked.

'Sir?'

'I said, aren't you going to let us in?'

'What do you want to come in here for, sir?'

'That's not for you to worry about, is it?' Helix said.

'I'm not sure I can admit anyone,' said the Guard, his face expressionless.

'In case you hadn't noticed, we are all Persons,' I told him pointedly. 'If we want to come in, that's all you need to know.'

'That'll do, Vector,' said Helix.

The Guard still showed no sign of moving aside. But then we heard another voice, and a second Guard appeared beside the first. He had a badge of rank on his shoulder.

'Ah, Dyne!' said Helix. 'What's going on here! Why hasn't this fellow let us in?'

Dyne was a compact Creature, spruce and self-possessed. He had a narrow face with small, sharp eyes, and his almost-black hair was cut very short and lay flat across his scalp. He creased his face into a smile that didn't seem natural to it.

'Sorry, sir,' he said. 'Of course you can come in. Ignorant, some of these fellows are, just ignorant.' And then, to the Guard, with a change of expression and tone:

'Get out of the way, you! Let the Persons in!'

The Guard looked resentful. It was obvious that he'd been obeying orders and Dyne had overruled them. But he backed away. Dyne gestured to us to enter. The door slid to behind us. I felt a moment's uneasiness as it did so. But Dyne was smiling again.

'I do apologize,' he said. 'Some of our fellows is so used to dealing with Creatures that they forget how to pay respect to quality. Now, sir, what can I do for you?'

'I said, what's going on?' Helix asked again, sharply. 'Why are

29

half the Colony's craft parked here? Who said they could be taken from the Precinct?'

'Well, now,' said Dyne. 'In point of fact it was me what authorized it, being, as you might remember, sir, if you was to put your mind to it, Head Guard and Craft Manager.'

'I do remember,' Helix said. 'But I don't remember that your duties extended to this.'

Dyne ignored this remark.

'To answer your other question,' he said, 'what's going on is a meeting of the Guards' Social Club. Which is duly authorized by the Regent, and which I am chairman of. And which I took the liberty of facilitating by putting craft at the disposal of.' Though his tone remained ingratiating, there was a hint of challenge behind it. 'And now, sir,' he went on, 'perhaps you'll do me the honour of informing me what *you* are doing here.'

'A Person doesn't have to explain himself to a Guard!' I broke in indignantly. But Helix hushed me.

'I just brought two of my pupils to see the Survey Station,' he said.

'Ah, yes, sir.' Dyne's voice was regretful. 'I'm sorry there's nothing really to see these days. The remaining equipment was put into store.' He met a look from Helix and added, 'With authority, sir. From the Regent. So I regret very much as how you've had a wasted journey.'

'Let's not talk about wasted journeys,' Helix said. 'To start with, we'd like to go up to the dome.'

I thought Dyne didn't look too pleased about this. But his attitude of helpful servility didn't change. 'Certainly, sir,' he said. The other Guard was still lingering nearby, and Dyne called him over.

'Tell the meeting,' he said, 'that I am busy with distinguished visitors, and will return to the chair when circumstances allows, which will be as soon as possible.'

'We can look around without you, Dyne, if you'd rather go back to your meeting,' Helix said. But obviously that was not what Dyne wanted. He accompanied us up to the dome, which had windows all round it and was echoingly bare. From a gallery Harmony and I looked out across the city to the silvery Towers, whose tops were now catching a glint of sun and seeming to float clear of the ground. We pointed out to each other the river, the Stumps, and such few landmarks as we could identify, while Dyne waited patiently and Helix stood unusually silent, with a puzzled expression on his face.

'And now,' he said to Dyne a few minutes later when we had seen all there was to see, 'I'd just like to have a look in the other rooms of this building.'

Dyne met his eye.

'I'm sorry, sir,' he said in a voice which for a Guard was almost soft. 'I'm sorry, sir, but all the rooms is locked up except the one where we're having our meeting. Our social club meeting.'

'You can open them, can't you?'

'Forgive me, sir, but begging your permission to say so, I'm the chairman of the meeting now in progress, and I'd be grateful for your kind consideration if you was to bring your tour to an end and let me get back to it.'

'You *have* taken up quite a lot of his time, Helix,' Harmony remarked. And indeed it seemed to me that Helix had been showing less than his usual consideration. But he was unmoved.

'I should like to see inside the other rooms,' he repeated.

There were some seconds of silence. I had the impression that a battle of wills was going on. Then Dyne said, his voice even quieter:

'I don't have the combination to open them, sir.'

'Somebody must have it.'

'No, sir. Nobody here.'

'Then call the Towers and get it, will you?' Helix's voice had softened to match Dyne's, and each of them spoke with quiet implacability.

'I can't at present. The caller's out of order.'

'*The* caller? You mean there's only one caller?'

'Yes, sir.'

'And why hasn't it been repaired?'

'The Equipment Guard's off duty, sir. And his deputy's not well. He has pains in his back, I'm told.'

'This is monstrous, Dyne.'

'No, sir, it's unfortunate, that's all. I repeat, sir, I'm sorry you can't see in them rooms, but there it is, there's no way I can oblige you. Though there's nothing to see if you *did* get inside.'

'I shall have to report this to the Regent,' Helix said.

'Of course, sir. As you wish.'

Helix had lost. There were subdued undertones of chagrin in his voice and of triumph in Dyne's.

'We'll walk down the stairs instead of taking the climb,' Helix said. A room opened out of each side of the staircase on each of the four floors, but every door was immovably closed. From one of the rooms we thought we heard voices, but Dyne pronounced firmly that he couldn't hear a thing.

The lowest storey, which extended farther than the others, included some kind of assembly hall, the door of which was open and guarded. Through it we could see the ends of several rows of seated, uniformed Guards. As Dyne showed us out of the building we heard their voices raised in a rapid, rhythmic chant.

'That's just our fellows singing,' Dyne said. 'Keeping themselves amused, I dare say, until I go back to them.'

'Singing?' I repeated. That seemed to me an absurd term for such painful cacophony.

'Yes. Social club meetings always include what we call a bit of a singsong. Of course, it wouldn't appeal to Persons, being that much more musical than we are, but the fellows enjoys it.'

'Of course,' Helix said. And when Dyne, still at once obsequious and unyielding, had shown us out, he told us: 'That was a marching song.'

I didn't understand the term.

'Men used to use it for setting a rhythm,' Helix explained, 'so they could walk in step with each other.'

'What did they want to do that for?'

'One of Helix's famous old Creature customs,' Harmony said mischievously.

'A sinister one, actually,' said Helix. 'They used to march in step when they were going to war. And don't say I haven't told you what that meant.'

'Yes, I know what war meant,' I said. 'But it was disastrous, wasn't it? It didn't do anyone any good.'

'It certainly didn't. Wars were what brought the Creatures to the wretched state they're in now. I don't much care for hearing warlike sounds.'

'But there's no one to go to war against, now,' I said.

'Us?' suggested Harmony quietly.

'Oh, no, that's absurd,' I said. 'Creatures can't do anything. Half-starved, half-human, ignorant, unorganized....'

'Most Creatures can't do anything,' said Helix. 'But it could be different with the Guards. To a large extent they run the system, after all.'

'But they *are* only Guards,' I said. 'They're only here to serve us. They owe it to us that they're not out on the street in rags like the rest. It's our society, after all. We're the superiors.'

'They outnumber us by two to one,' Helix said. 'Three hundred Persons, six hundred Guards.'

'And a hundred thousand Creatures,' added Harmony.

'However many there are,' I said, 'surely neither Guards nor ordinary Creatures could run a society. They haven't the gift of reason. They can't do the things we do.'

'They can't understand philosophy or higher mathematics, certainly,' said Helix. 'And you've just heard an example of their singing. It's not what *we* would call singing, to say the least. They don't spend all day playing the Dimension Game, either. But maybe they could run a society on their own lines.'

'I think that's ridiculous,' I declared firmly. 'The Guards are loyal. They respect us. All they want to do is give satisfaction.'

'Do you think that's true of Dyne?' Helix asked.

I was silent. Dyne's obstinacy had been disconcerting.

'As you know,' Helix said, 'I think that ultimately this is the Creatures' planet. Our job here should be to help them up from the state they're in now. We don't achieve that by playing the Dimension Game. But I don't believe it would be achieved by leaving the Guards in charge, either. And whatever I think of the society we've got, I reckon we must protect it. So I shall talk to the Regent about what we've just seen.'

Helix didn't offer the tiller either to Harmony or myself on the way back. His expression was preoccupied. He took the most direct route and hardly said a word.

'And the best time for speaking to the Regent is now,' he

remarked, when we had stepped from the craft, walked across the roof of the Central Tower, and returned our hardly-used breathers and goggles to the dispenser.

We went straight down to the main lounge, where we expected to find the Regent. As a rule it was easy enough to talk to her. Anyone could do it. The best way was to catch her at a suitable break in the Game. Then, if you had a request to make, she would listen patiently and help you if she could.

Everyone knew Aria hadn't really wanted to be Regent, but everyone knew also that somebody had to have the last word on the minor problems that arose, even in a colony as smooth-running as ours. Aria had accepted election, to the relief of all the other Persons who might have been asked to serve if she hadn't. And everyone accepted Aria's decisions, because everyone knew that abiding by decisions was necessary for a civilized way of life. Nobody wanted squabbles or arguments; besides, such things wasted time and kept you from the Game. So for the five years of her term Aria was in unquestioned charge.

But today she wasn't at her usual table in the Game Lounge. In fact there was a subdued and uncharacteristic air of flurry and excitement.

'Where is she?' Helix asked Tangent, one of the seniors she usually played with.

'She's in the office.'

'In the office! A private interview?'

'Something more than that, I think,' Tangent said. 'A rush message came on the caller, and she hurried to the office at once. That was twenty minutes ago. She hasn't come out yet.'

'A rush message. From where?'

'Well, Helix, you can guess as much as any of us. Everybody's speculating.'

'I shall go straight in there,' Helix said.

They stared at him. It was not good manners to interrupt the Regent on the rare occasions when she conducted business from the office. A Person who had generously taken on the duties of Regent was entitled to privacy if required. It would be unPersonlike to intrude.

But then, Helix was not always Personlike. On this occasion he gestured to Harmony and myself to go with him. The combination for the Regent's door was known to everyone, so Helix keyed it and we went in.

The Regent was just switching off her caller. She was a calm, elegant Person, a full woman with the prestige of having successfully borne a child, back Home some years ago. She had come through the fertile phase now, and was fully devoted to Personlike pursuits – she composed aerotronic music, and was at the top table in the Dimension Game – except when her duties as Regent kept her from them.

This was the first time I had ever seen her excited.

'Helix!' she cried. 'And you two as well! You're the first to hear the news. The relief ship! We were beginning to think it was never coming. And here it is!'

For a moment even Helix forgot what he had to say. The relief ship! Its arrival was the most important thing that ever happened on Earth. It meant news from Home, supplies of goods that were scarce here, new members for the Colony. For some people here it meant a return to the Home they hadn't seen in years.

'It came through the time warp and into contact half an hour ago,' Aria said. 'It'll be in parking orbit by mid-evening. We'll have the ferry in operation at dawn. I must get a message to Dyne as soon as I've told the seniors.'

'Actually, Regent,' said Helix, 'there's something I'd like to tell you before we get involved with the relief ship.' And he launched rapidly into an account of what had happened at the Survey Station.

But Aria obviously didn't wish to listen. She tapped her fingers impatiently on her desk.

'Yes, yes, I know all about the Guards' Social Club,' she said. 'It was properly authorized.' She seemed unimpressed by the mention of locked doors, and was only interested in the fact that Dyne appeared to be out of contact through the breakdown of the caller.

'If it's not repaired, I'll send a craft for him right away,' she said. 'We need him to organize the ferry. I can't think what we'd do without Dyne. He really is invaluable.'

And she turned to the keyboard beside her to call in the seniors.

'I know how things are, Regent,' said Helix, 'but what I've just told you could be very important. More so, even, than the arrival of the relief ship.'

'Come now, Helix,' Aria said. 'That's going a bit far.' And then, 'Very well, by all means we'll discuss it at length. But not until the relief ship's gone.'

She touched a dozen keys, gave some swift instructions on the caller, and sat back, still looking pleased and excited.

'The seniors will be here in half a minute,' she said. 'Won't they be delighted! Won't *everybody* be delighted! The relief ship at last!'

Her eye fell on Harmony.

'And, Harmony, my dear! You'll be going Home! Perhaps in a year or two you'll be a mother. A viable child, I hope. There's a very good chance, you know. Some of us are lucky. *I* was.... Aren't you thrilled?'

'Frankly,' said Harmony, 'no.'

Aria looked at her incredulously. But there wasn't time for this shocking declaration to sink in. The office door opened, the seniors filed in and stood expectantly in a half-circle.

'It's great news!' Aria began.

Helix signalled to Harmony and me. We slipped quietly out of the office behind the seniors' backs. Until Harmony spoke, I'd been full of excitement myself. The relief ship! Through the time warp and in contact! Parking orbit tonight! The ferry operating tomorrow morning! For a few unthinking moments I was almost bursting to give the news to Cadenza and the boys. And then the realization struck me. I had discovered how I felt about Harmony just in time to lose her.

Chapter Four

The bustle of the next few days was such as hadn't been seen in the Colony since our own arrival four years earlier. The ferry made three trips daily to the ship, and each time it returned there were fresh excitements. More new arrivals to be disembarked, more greetings between old friends and acquaintances, more goods and delicacies from Home, and more news.

The news of course was six months old; but without the arrival of the ship we would have heard nothing, since communications couldn't cross the time warp. There was news of who had been persuaded to take over the administration, of the births of viable babies (none too many of these), of who had been winning the Dimension Game championships and which techniques had led them to victory. The ship's captain and crew, a rather unPersonlike lot, were welcomed and fêted in a sudden rush of social events; only a few old colonial hands with no interest in Home and no wish to go back continued calmly to play the Game in a corner of the unaccustomedly noisy lounge.

To the young Persons the arrival of half a dozen juniors of the minimum permitted age for a stay on Earth was of special interest. They seemed incredibly immature (though presumably no more so than we had been four years previously) and eager for our friendship. Inquiries were made on both sides about prowess at the Game, and it seemed that most of them were even less advanced than I was.

'That will be nice for you, won't it, Vector?' Cadenza said kindly. 'You won't be the weakest player in the whole Colony any more.'

'You don't think I care about that, do you?' I retorted. 'The Game isn't everything.'

'Well, it isn't for me or Harmony,' said Cadenza, who was also going Home and looking forward to it. 'But you poor boys must find what compensations you can.'

She sounded unbearably smug. I was glad she was going. But I tried not to think about Harmony's departure. I was doing my best to believe that the extraordinary sensations I'd felt on board the open craft were just a temporary effect of too much light and air.

The ship had only ten days of turn-round time before it left again for Annulus. On the last of these days, Harmony and Cadenza and the other Homebound passengers would embark. And then, I told myself, I would return to normal Personhood. If possible I would be a more orthodox Person than before. I would try harder at the Game, especially since I would no longer be at the very foot of the table. Life would be more agreeable when I had moved up a few places.

In the meantime, I resolved not to upset myself by contact with Harmony. For two days after the ship's arrival I managed not to speak to her at all. On the third day, restless and uneasy, I went for a walk by myself in the Precinct, and found her sitting alone on a seat, in a quiet corner beyond the softlight fountains. She looked up as I joined her and gave me half a smile. I had a strong impression that she had been crying. And instantly my resolution shattered. The unPersonlike feelings of the craft trip returned more strongly than ever, propelled by a sudden charge of sympathy and affection. Without really intending it, I put an arm round her and drew her towards me.

She resisted me at first. 'What's the use, Vector?' she said. 'I have to go Home, and you can't come with me. We shall only make ourselves miserable.'

But for the moment at least my feelings were at the other extreme from reason and responsibility. I didn't say anything but drew her closer still. And at once her resistance collapsed and she was returning my embrace and kissing me on the lips.

I knew about kissing, of course. I knew it was a standard technique of courtship, strongly recommended as a preliminary to those Persons back Home who were charged with the task of maintaining the population. But I hadn't actually done it, or had it done to me, before; and the depth of feeling it released astonished me. We clung together for some minutes, and our lips and tongues and hands seemed to speak to each other and to have ways of communication that we hadn't known about.

Harmony drew back. She was weeping again. Then she sat up straight and dried her eyes.

'I want to *stay*!' she declared. 'I want to break out of the Precinct and go into the world and do things and never play the Game again and find out and find out and find out. And, to start with, I want to find out what happened to Melody. And I don't want to go Home and be paired with some specially selected male and have a viable baby if I'm lucky and a series of non-viable ones if I'm not. If I'm to pair, I'd rather it was with you, Vector. And I'd rather it was here on Earth.'

I was delighted and alarmed at the same time. My feelings in fact were in a state of total confusion. But I took some kind of a grip on myself.

'Listen,' I said. 'We're Persons, after all. We're supposed to be free. We don't have to do what we don't want to do. Let's both go to Aria tomorrow morning and tell her what you've just told me, and then surely she'll let you stay.'

'I'm not so sure,' Harmony said. 'But we can try.' And the next morning we both presented ourselves at the office, where Aria was spending an unusual amount of time organizing things during the relief ship's visit. The Captain was with her: a heavily-built Person with – surely – a hint of down above the mouth and about the chin. Aria was distracted, and more distant than usual.

'Tell me briefly what you want, dear,' she said to Harmony. 'I'm sure it will be all right.'

But when Harmony explained, her expression changed.

'Nonsense!' she exclaimed. 'Marriageable girls go Home. You can't expect me to change that. They're *needed*.'

'But I've thought about it,' Harmony said. 'It's not just a whim, it's serious. I truly don't want to go. And I'm ... fond of Vector.'

'Really, my dear!' Aria said. 'Don't you think you're being just a little absurd? Aren't you perhaps in a slightly emotional state? Don't worry about it. We full women get like that sometimes; it's a price we pay for being privileged. When you're safely Home with the prospect of a baby you'll feel differently, I can assure you.'

'Of course you will!' the Captain said. He'd been eyeing Harmony appreciatively. 'A pretty girl like you! You'll be popular on Annulus, I can tell you. And if they have any trouble in finding a pair for you, I don't mind volunteering myself!'

Aria quelled him with a look. Harmony ignored the interruption and went on,

'We're always told we can do what we want. And what I want to do is stay!'

Aria became severe.

'I've told you, Harmony, it's out of the question. Your duty is to go Home. Society needs what you can contribute. And suppose you were to ... get together with Vector here, why, anything might happen. There could be a most unsuitable result. Babies must be born at Home, where the atmosphere is right for them and they can have proper care and the best possible start in life. Anything else would be unthinkable!'

'But....' Harmony began.

'No, dear, I won't hear another word. There are no two ways about it. You must go and that's that!'

'Could I go too?' I asked.

'Definitely not, Vector. There are no places for young males, I'm afraid. And there are more people who've completed their tour than we can find room for on the ship. Some of them are feeling disappointed as it is. It would be an outrage to give you preference over them.'

Then her expression softened a little.

'I'm sorry,' she said. 'I do understand. But I'm afraid I can't help you. And I'm sure that in a year's time you'll both be wondering what all the fuss was about.'

'Not I,' said Harmony, and stalked from the room.

'Nor I,' I said, surprising myself; and I followed.

It didn't occur to me that Aria's ruling could be defied, but for the time being at least I felt that I didn't care about propriety and that the best thing we could do was to make what we could of our last few days.

And during those days I spent as much time with Harmony as I could. It was a period that was at once sad, exciting and totally perplexing. The new language of the body and the emotions was

40

one which we did not understand, and which appeared to be alien to those around us. We had never seen Persons embrace as we embraced. We knew about conception and childbirth, and about genetics and the genetic problems that had made the continuance of our species doubtful, but we weren't prepared for the over-whelming emotion, the sense of involvement and commitment, that went along with the physical sensations.

Helix was unaccountably absent from his rooms during most of this time, and the other seniors of the Colony could give us little help. A few of them had experienced parenthood, but those who could spare time from the Game to talk to us did not seem to have any very vivid recollection of what had led up to it. They didn't regard the subject as particularly interesting, and the actual bringing up of children was a community undertaking to which as individual parents they had contributed little.

The general view was the same as Aria's: that Harmony and I would grow out of our devotion, and that in the meantime we should take matters more calmly. One or two of the seniors suggested that we should talk to Rhombus, the Colony's medical man; but Rhombus had left, as he did every year, for a late vacation at the Summer Valley, and in any case we didn't see how he could have anything to propose except the operation.

There was little we could do except talk to each other and engage in the tentative embraces which we found both delightful and alarming. The Colony was not equipped for privacy; physical contact beyond the ritual hand-touch was regarded by Persons as gross and embarrassing; and we ourselves felt a little ashamed of our passion.

The quietest place we could find was the little area beyond the softlight fountains, among the ornamental bushes. Here we could sit, holding hands and experiencing from time to time the mysterious joys of kissing; but we could never count on being alone for long enough to feel secure. This corner was not far from the path that led to the Guards' quarters; and whereas Persons would at least look tactfully aside, the Guards who occasionally passed by on their way to or from their barracks felt no such inhibition. One evening we heard a scuffling sound and realized that a Guard was peering at us from a well-concealed hiding place behind a clump of bushes. The incident had a chilling and miserable effect, making us feel we were up to something disreputable.

This effect was partly dispersed when Node came by a little later on his way from duty at the guardroom, and was hailed by Harmony. Node observed our affection for each other at once. ·

'What it is to be young!' he remarked; and, however simple and obvious his reactions, I had a disconcerting impression that he was better able to sympathize with us than our fellow-Persons. But he couldn't give us any advice.

'It needs someone brighter than me to sort *that* out,' he said when we'd told him of our dilemma. 'If I was you, I'd ask Mr Helix. Now *he's* a clever gentleman, and a deep one, too.'

But that was just what we couldn't do. There was still no sign of Helix.

'I wish I knew where he is,' Harmony would say each day; and it wasn't until the night before the ship was due to leave that she met me in the Precinct with the news that she had just seen him on the way to his rooms.

'We must talk to him at once while we have the chance,' she said. 'I feel he's our last hope.'

We walked over to Tower One, where the senior Persons lived, and went up the climb to Helix's floor. On the way to his rooms we passed old Cosine's studio, from which we could hear the un-melodious sound of some reconstructed Earth-style noise-making device. Cosine had been busy for years building weird instruments out of wood or tortured metal; he had even trained a few unfortunate Guards to blow, scrape or beat them into activity, and talked of forming what he called an 'orchestra' to play old Creature music. Most Persons hoped they would never have to hear it. But this evening neither Harmony nor I could spare as much as a smile for poor Cosine's harmless dreams.

'I'm glad to see you at last,' Harmony said when Helix had admitted us. 'You must have been very busy.'

'Yes.'

'You're often busy in your own mysterious way, aren't you, Helix?'

'Yes.'

Helix didn't seem inclined to tell us anything about his activities, and I don't suppose Harmony expected him to. She went on,

'You know the position Vector and I are in, don't you?'

'Yes.'

'Helix, can you help us?'

'If you mean, can I persuade Aria to change her mind, I'm afraid the answer is that I can't. As Regent she's made certain promises to Annulus. One of them is to ensure the observance of established colonial customs, and one of *those* is that women go Home for childbearing. Aria's not the sort of Person to go back on a promise. I expect she believes in the custom herself, anyway. She went Home to have her own child.'

'What do you think I should do, then?'

'I don't see what you *can* do, Harmony. I'm sorry, but there it is.'

Harmony was silent for a moment. Then she said quietly, 'Suppose I just refused to go. Simply and absolutely refused. Do you think they'd put me on the ship by brute force?'

Helix considered this, then said, 'No, I don't think so. I've never heard of brute force being used against a Person. For that matter, I've never heard of a Person putting authority into a position where it would need to consider using brute force.'

'Well, then, perhaps that's what I'll do. The ship won't wait long, you know. With all those people on board and a tight schedule, they won't want to waste time arguing with me. And once it's gone, there won't be another for four years.'

'Harmony,' said Helix, 'I'm sorry, but speaking as your friend I can only give you one piece of advice. Don't do anything so rash!'

'It's not all *that* rash. A bit unPersonlike, perhaps, but why should I let that worry me?'

'You mustn't do it.'

'Why not, Helix, why not?'

'Well, for one thing, I think the safest place for a young woman just now is on a ship going Home to Annulus. For another, have you considered what would happen *after* you refused?'

'Aria would be furious,' said Harmony. 'But she wouldn't actually punish me.'

'She wouldn't lock you up, that's true. Whatever its faults, the Colony is civilized. But do you suppose she could just let you and

Vector come happily together? She couldn't, you know. It's not just a matter of letting you get away with a gross breach of propriety. There'll be something else in her mind as well.'

'I know,' said Harmony. 'She told us. She's afraid we might start a baby.' Her voice was bitter. 'A baby born here in the Colony. A major scandal, with inquiries back Home and the Regent accused of negligence. Oh yes, I can scan her mind perfectly. But that wouldn't happen, you know, not till we were ready. We're not *so* ignorant.'

'Anyway,' I said, 'if she didn't lock either of us up, how could Aria prevent us from being together?'

'I can tell you that without the slightest hesitation,' Helix said. 'First, she'd ask you both for a promise not to associate with each other.'

'We wouldn't give it,' said Harmony promptly.

'All right, so you wouldn't give it. Then Vector would have to bear the brunt. It's his misfortune that he's a male, and males matter less to the community. Aria would give you a choice, Vector, between two alternatives. One is to have the operation.'

'Oh, no!' Harmony exclaimed.

'But then I wouldn't be a full male,' I said.

'Exactly. That's the whole idea. Well, you know, a great many males in the Colony do have the operation of their own free will, and they all say they don't regret it; it saves a lot of pointless yearning.'

'It's out of the question!' Harmony declared.

'The other alternative,' said Helix, 'is for Vector to be ejected from the Colony and take his chance outside.'

My heart suddenly began to thump.

'But that's outrageous!' Harmony cried. 'Aria can't punish *him* for what *I* do!'

'He's expendable,' said Helix. 'You're not.'

'How can you be so sure that's what Aria would do?' I asked.

'Because there was a similar situation a few years ago. A male Person became involved with a female and was given the choice I've just outlined. That was Polygon. He chose to go outside.'

'And what happened to him?'

'I can't tell you.'

44

'I'd rather go outside myself than have Vector put out,' said Harmony.

'That wouldn't be easy. Juniors aren't allowed to go out, least of all junior females. And there'd be no point anyway, because you'd still be separated from Vector.... Unless of course Vector were to go outside as well.'

'Unless I went outside as well!' I echoed. And terror descended on me. To go outside, among the primitive and probably savage Creatures! It would be a death sentence, and probably a sentence to death by some horrible means: violence, starvation, disease. That was not a fate I could face. The wild ideas I'd been entertaining during the last few days suddenly ebbed away, leaving me once again a cautious Person.

'I wouldn't ask Vector to do that,' said Harmony.

There was silence. This was my opportunity to leap in with an offer to dare anything for her. And just for a moment I experienced another violent swing of feeling, a reckless impulse to do just that. But it passed, and I said nothing.

'You're right, I suppose, Helix,' Harmony said. 'There's no point in my resisting. I may as well accept what has to happen. I must go Home to Annulus.'

I sat ashamed but still silent.

'So that's that,' Harmony said, with an obvious attempt at brightness.

'I would like to be with you anywhere, Harmony,' I said feebly, 'but....'

'But she isn't asking you to, Vector,' said Helix.

'No, I'm not,' Harmony agreed. She laughed, rather too lightly. 'Poor Vector. You'd never make a story-book hero.'

'A what?'

'A story-book hero.'

'I don't suppose he knows what that means,' said Helix.

'No, I don't.'

'Let's show him,' said Harmony. 'I suppose it takes our minds off our troubles.' She picked something up from a table. 'There, Vector, do you know what this is?'

'Of course I do,' I said. 'It's the Book. Helix showed it to the group once before. Don't you remember, Helix? There used to be lots of them, you said. An old Creature way of communicating.'

'That's right. A lost skill. But you didn't see inside it, did you? Take a look now. This is how you open it.'

After demonstrating, Helix passed the Book across to me. It consisted of numerous sheets of a thin white material, fastened into a hard grainy brown cover in such a way that you could turn them over one at a time. On both sides of each sheet were rows of black marks. It was the first time I had seen what I came to know as writing, and at the time it didn't strike me as particularly important or interesting. My mind was still torn between fear of going outside and shame at my own timidity.

'One of the Guards found it in a ruined building,' Helix said. 'He didn't know what it was, and gave it to me.'

'And Helix knew, of course,' said Harmony. 'It's a book of stories.'

'What are stories?'

'They're ... descriptions of events that never happened.'

'You mean lies?'

'No. They're not lies, because nobody ever thinks they *did* happen. They're about things that if they *had* happened would have been interesting.'

'I don't see the point.'

'Vector has probably never heard a story,' Helix said gently. 'There's no reason why he should. Persons don't, you know, Harmony, unless they happen to associate with oddities like me.'

'Tell him one, then,' Harmony said. 'Tell him about the people who all fell asleep for years and years.'

'All right,' Helix said. And by decoding the black marks on the whitish leaves of the Book he produced an extraordinary account of how a female Creature, improbably stated to be beautiful, was put to sleep for a hundred years by an act of pointless malice, and was then awakened by a kiss from a young male. The whole thing was obviously absurd.

'A Creature couldn't sleep for a hundred years,' I said. 'Guards are Creatures, and they only sleep a few hours at a time. They don't even *live* a hundred years. And then to be awakened by a kiss. . . .'

'But, Vector,' said Harmony, 'I feel as if something like that had happened to *me*, just these last few days, since we began to feel as we do about each other. It's as if I'd been brought to life.'

Wild as it was, that remark seemed to make some kind of sense. When we'd been high over the city on the craft without goggles or breathers; when I'd put my arms round Harmony and felt that strange mixture of physical excitement and emotional outflow ... yes, it was like arriving in an enhanced form of life, heady and perilous. Harmony went on:

'The girl in that story was a princess, and the young man was a prince.'

'What's a princess and a prince?'

'A kind of regent, I think.'

'But regents are old. Aria's a regent and she's old. And Cosine before her was even older.'

'These were young, very special, very brave and loving people.'

'People?' I said. 'They weren't people, they were Creatures.'

'You sound like Cadenza. When Helix told us this story before, she was with us, and all she said was, "Fancy being kissed by a nasty, hairy Creature!"'

'Well, yes, it's a bit disgusting, isn't it?'

'You wouldn't think so if you were a Creature,' Helix said.

'Vector,' said Harmony, sighing, 'in these old tales there were often heroes – young men who would risk their lives if necessary to rescue their princesses.'

'I suppose we're different now,' I said.

'Yes, I know risking your life is disapproved of in the Colony. Lives can't be spared. And I know Helix and I have all the wrong ideas, from a Person's point of view. We're not desirable company for you, Vector. Oh well, so far as it concerns me, your problem's almost over. You can go back to being a nice orthodox Person. You'll forget me before long.'

I saw that she was on the point of tears.

'I don't think Vector's ready for being a hero,' said Helix. 'Not yet. Not quite.'

'Of course not,' Harmony said in a steady voice, controlled with obvious effort. 'Excuse me, Helix. I must go now. I don't suppose I shall see you again. Good-bye.'

'Good-bye, Harmony,' Helix said. 'I wish you well. Aria's probably right, you know. You'll feel quite differently when....'

'Oh, spare me that sort of talk!' Harmony burst out; and then, shamefaced, 'I'm sorry I was rude, Helix. Thank you for your advice. Good-bye again.'

She walked out of the room. I looked at Helix questioningly.

'Go after her, Vector,' he said. 'She needs you. There's nothing I can do.'

I caught Harmony up and took her hand. Without saying anything we went down the climb and out into the Precinct. The seat we usually occupied, between the ornamental bushes and the softlight fountains, was free and there was no one around. We sat there for a long time, silently holding hands. Through the transparent roof, far above, the moon could be clearly seen, bright and almost full. Harmony's face was outlined in the clear pale light. Her high forehead and aura of fine hair seemed agonizingly beautiful to me. Her eyes were wide, deep and remote; I knew that beyond the contact of hands she didn't want to be touched.

After a long time she said, 'Well, that was it. It was brief, and now it's over.'

There was another silence; then, 'Don't come to the ferry to see me go, Vector. I couldn't bear that. Just say good-bye to me now.'

I leaned towards her to kiss her. She responded, but not with the eagerness of other evenings. I had a sense that she was abstracted; was distant already.

'I must say good-bye to Node as well,' she said. 'It wouldn't do to go away for ever without a word to him.' And then, with passion, 'Oh, it's absurd, it's impossible! Why must I? Why should I? Why can't you....? Why...?'

'Why what?'

'Nothing,' she said. 'Good-bye, Vector. Good-bye.'

Chapter Five

I slept poorly that night. It wasn't so much the thought that I would never see Harmony again; that had not yet sunk in. What afflicted me was bitter shame at my own cowardice, made worse by a guilty sense of relief. I lay awake for a long time; then, after two or three hours' uneasy sleep, I woke again with my stomach churning anxiously. It was still not morning, but I knew that I couldn't sleep any more and the only way to calm myself was to get up and walk around.

I found my feet taking me over the bridgeway that led from my Tower to the Precinct walls. There was a broad walk along the top of the walls, with a waist-high parapet to make sure you didn't fall off; and you could complete a circuit of the Precinct in about half an hour. It wasn't a popular activity at any time; it involved going out through an airlock and (if you followed the safety rules) wearing breather and goggles. Few Persons were fond of walking, and even fewer wanted to look out from those parapets at the dismal sight of the city.

In the half-light there was no need for goggles, and I decided I could do without a breather, too. The sky was mostly clear, but far to the east, over the mountains, a rosy light was refracted from a bank of cloud. In front of me, the outlines of the city's sprawling streets were still blurred. The air, as always on Earth, was rich; a faint, sweet exhalation of decay rose into my nostrils. And suddenly the uncontrollable flow of feeling which had led me into so many unPersonlike reactions gathered force again and possessed me completely; and this time I knew I must let it have its way.

I loved Harmony. She was willing to refuse to return to Annulus. More than that, she was willing to go outside. Very well, then; if going outside was the only way we could be together I was willing to go outside too. With each other's support we could go anywhere, do anything. Outside there was squalor and danger, no doubt; but outside also there was rich invigorating air and the light of day; rain and wind and sunshine. Who wanted to stay in the dull, narrow, air-and-light-conditioned safety of the Colony, passing endless time with the Dimension Game? Not we. We were strong and healthy; there was a good chance that we would survive outside. And if we didn't – well, I thought rashly, better a short time together than a long dreary existence apart.

I wasn't a different Person since last night, I knew. I would have many more times of fear; I knew that, too. But my decision was made, and I was freed and strengthened by it.

Looking down from the wall, I could now see figures straggling up the approach road which led to the main gate: Creatures coming to line up for work. Feeble lights flickered here and there in dwellings whose outlines were becoming discernible in the growing light. Behind me, most of the Precinct still slept under its huge transparent canopy. But over at the terminal on the Central Tower roof, there was light and activity already in preparation for the departure of the ferry, whose blunt-nosed bulk could be clearly seen. I looked at the time. In barely an hour now, that ferry would leave on the final trip of the relief ship's present visit, taking Persons on board for the passage to Annulus.

I must try to make sure that Harmony didn't go on it after all. But I had left things desperately late. It couldn't be long before the passengers were called for embarkation.

I ran back to the bridgeway, fidgeting at the brief delay caused by the airlock. Into my own Tower, down the climb to ground level, out into the Precinct, running across the ornamental garden with a couple of early servants stopping to stare at me. Into Tower Three, where the women's quarters were. The climb slow to arrive; myself uttering curses in Creature, learned as a boy from Node. Up the stairs instead; hurrying breathless along the corridor to Harmony's room. And the door stood wide. No Harmony, none of her possessions; the room was vacant as if she'd never been there at all.

I stood panting, telling myself for a moment that I might have come to the wrong room, but knowing I hadn't. I turned to see Cadenza in the doorway. Instead of the gown of cool, smooth, shiny material which female Persons usually wore, she was wearing practical dress: brief, neat and becoming.

'You naughty boy, Vector!' she said archly. 'A male in the women's quarters, and at this hour of the morning, too!'

'Where is she?' I demanded.

'Harmony? Don't be in such a panic, Vector. I expect she's gone across to the departure lounge.'

'Is it time?'

'It soon will be.'

'I must see her. At once.'

'There'll be time, Vector. No need to hurry. You can walk over there with me.'

'Where are all her things, Cadenza?'

'I expect they've been collected. You *are* in a state.'

I didn't wait for Cadenza. I ran out, ran down the stairs, ran across the Precinct to the Central Tower, hurried up to the ferry terminal. No sign of Harmony along the way. I was worried now in case she had already boarded the ferry; if she had, it was hard to see how I could get her off it.

She wasn't in the departure lounge. The Guards at the gate to the ferry denied having seen her. Nobody had gone on board yet, they said. That was something. But if she wasn't on the ferry, or in the departure lounge, or in her own Tower, where on Earth was she?

A new cause for alarm struck me. She'd been determined not to go. Suppose ... just suppose she'd taken the most drastic of all ways out? I'd just come down from the walls; and on the outside they descended, sheer and smooth, for thirty metres to the paving below. They were designed to be unassailable by any kind of barbarian. Anyone who jumped off them would be taking a quick route to ... cessation. The walls were two and a half kilometres round, and mostly deserted.

I was pondering this thought with horror when Cadenza arrived in the departure lounge.

'It wasn't very Personlike to dash away like that, Vector,' she said reproachfully.

'She isn't here! Harmony isn't here!' I said.

'I expect she's saying good-bye to somebody. Although I should have thought' – there was a note of sweet malice in Cadenza's voice – 'that if she had a special farewell to make, it would be to you.'

I muttered more Earth curses. There was no point in running around the Precinct looking for Harmony. All I could do was hope that my fears were misplaced and wait here to intercept her when she arrived. I stationed myself at the entry door to the lounge. It was filling up now. The passenger list had appeared on the wall indicator display, and as people checked in their names blacked out, one by one. After a few minutes there were only ten or twelve scattered names of non-arrivals still showing on the panel. Harmony's was one of them.

There wasn't much time left for last-minute rebellion, and now that the embarkation procedure was smoothly under way I began to lose faith in that possibility. But another possibility had now suggested itself. Suppose she didn't come at all? A default of this kind was so unPersonlike, so unheard-of, that I found it hard at first to entertain the idea. Even Harmony herself had never suggested that she might fail to turn up for the ferry.

The bustle in the lounge increased. People were being seen off by their friends. Even the cool Persons showed signs of emotion, for few of those who were parting would ever see each other again. The three boys stood with Cadenza in a little group. They looked wistful, but she shone with satisfaction; for days she had been delighting in her new status as a potential mother. She was advising Secant to have the operation; the others, it seemed, were not in need of it.

Boarding began. One by one the passengers filed out through the gate. Their friends went the other way, towards the observation deck, from which they would be able to watch the ferry leave. The lounge emptied rapidly. Only four names were now displayed on the indicator; Harmony's was still one of them.

An announcement was made on the ceiling speaker and flashed on the notice-panel: it would be heard over every speaker and seen on every screen in the Precinct. Would these four Persons please check in at once? And in the next five minutes, three late and slightly flustered Persons arrived, to be rapidly dealt with and waved through the gate.

But still no Harmony. The idea that she might not appear at all seemed less and less incredible; began indeed to be a likelihood, though the thought of those high smooth walls still troubled me. I watched the desk Guard's lips move in front of his microphone as another announcement came over the speaker and was flashed on the wall-screen.

'Will Miss Harmony please report immediately to the ferry terminal,' it said. 'Miss Harmony, to the ferry terminal.'

Hardly anyone was left in the departure lounge now. There were a couple of members of the ship's crew and a handful of Guards, including Dyne, the Head Guard, who was also craft manager. And the Captain of the relief ship was there, too, talking in a corner with Aria and another of the Colony's seniors.

Their conversation ceased. Everyone was waiting now. The Captain glanced impatiently at the time and gestured to the desk Guard. A third announcement went out:

'Miss Harmony! Proceed to the terminal *at once*, please. The ferry is waiting!'

And a minute later Aria herself strode across to the microphone, and the speaker came alive with her irritated voice:

'Harmony! Where are you? Come to the terminal this minute! You're holding everyone up!'

The silence that followed was almost audible. Aria beckoned me across.

'Vector!' she said. 'As you see, there's no sign of Harmony. We know you're close to her. Have you any idea where she is?'

'Not the slightest,' I said.

'She was talking of not wanting to go Home,' said Aria thoughtfully. 'I'm beginning to wonder if she could have made some . . . some wild decision. But for a Person simply not to turn up is . . . well, it's outside my experience! You're quite sure you know nothing about it, Vector?'

'Nothing,' I said truthfully. 'I wouldn't have come if I hadn't expected to see her here.'

'Listen, Regent,' the Captain said. 'We're late already. Everyone else is on board and we're all set for take-off. How long do you expect me to wait for some silly girl?'

'Give me another five minutes, Captain,' Aria said. And a few seconds later an announcement was going out on all speakers and screens, calling on Persons and Guards alike to search the Precinct for Harmony.

'She could be ill, I suppose,' said Aria. 'Anyway, she'll soon be found. The Colony isn't very large, after all. There aren't many places where she could be.'

'Sneaked outside, perhaps?' the Captain suggested.

'Oh, no, surely she wouldn't do *that*! Besides, she'd have to pass the guardroom, and they have instructions that juniors mustn't go out.'

'You'd be surprised what kids can do when they set their minds to it,' the Captain said. 'If some of you Colonials had my experience of life. . . .'

'Quite,' said Aria coldly.

'The Guards is very keen, sir,' put in Dyne, who had come across to join the group. 'Nobody gets past that guardroom what shouldn't.'

'Could she have got her hands on a craft?' the Captain asked.

'She wouldn't know how to fly one.'

'She might,' I said unthinkingly.

'It's not all that difficult,' the Captain said. 'Any kid with a bit of common sense and enterprise could fly a craft.'

But a call from Dyne to the craft hangar brought the reply that no craft were missing.

'Sorry, Regent,' the Captain said. 'Ten minutes late now. I'm not going to keep everyone crowded in that lumbering old ferry any longer. I mean to be away and into the time warp by tonight.'

'She'll be found any moment now,' Aria said.

'Maybe, maybe not. Anyway, I think you told me she's seventeen, counting in Earth years. She'll still only be twenty-one when the next relief ship comes. Lots of time ahead of her.'

'Yes, but. . . .'

'I know what you're thinking,' the Captain said. 'Girls will be girls. Might get into trouble, eh? Oh, well, if you have any problems the doc will see you through.'

Aria looked outraged. But then the desk Guard hurried across.

'Your Highness! Your assistant just called. A message from Harmony! Keyed in during the night with a delay until now. It's just come up on the screen in your office. It says: "Gone outside permanently. Vector not involved. Regret trouble caused. Harmony." '

Aria sat down on the nearest chair.

'I can't believe it!' she said faintly.

'Well, there you are,' said the Captain. He sounded relieved. 'What did I tell you? You can't put anything past these kids.'

'But what are we going to do about it?'

'You can't do anything. Timed her message well, hasn't she? We're leaving now.' And then, more sympathetically, 'Don't look so worried, Regent. Worse things happen on other worlds. In fact it's happened here before now, hasn't it? Wherever there's a colony, there's someone that goes native. They won't be *too* upset about it on Annulus. A pity, I know, to lose a pretty girl like that; she looked a promising breeder, too. But keep calm and just let her go. She'll probably come back one of these days. Deserters often think better of it.'

Dyne broke in, with repressed fury.

'What *I* want to know,' he said, 'is how she got past the guardroom. For that to happen, just when I'd told you it couldn't. . . . It's too much!' He added, darkly, 'That's if she *did* get past the guardroom. What if she's just bluffing, eh? What if she's still inside?'

'There's nothing to be done about it now,' the Captain said firmly. 'Come along, Regent. Make your farewell speech to your passengers. And keep it brief, please. They'll be panting to get away.'

Aria sighed. 'I don't like this at all,' she said. 'You can keep that last announcement running if you like, Dyne. If Harmony can be found, I certainly want to see her, though it won't do much good at this stage. But if she's really gone outside, I suppose the Captain's right and there's no point in pursuing her; we'll just have to let her go. Oh, what a dreadful thing to happen!'

She went out through the gate to the ferry, with the Captain beside her. Dyne was muttering angrily to the desk Guard. It seemed to me to be a good idea to get away from him as quickly as possible. I hurried down the climb. Two or three Guards were on the ground floor of the Tower, opening and closing doors, and there were even a few Person faces peering vaguely along corridors and making some show of a search. I didn't think they would persist for long before returning to the Game.

Still, Dyne was not to be underestimated. I looked all round me as I strode out into the Precinct, in case I was being followed, but there was no sign of that. I was half-way between one Tower and another when I felt the tremor that meant the ferry had left. I looked up and could see it through the clear canopy, dwindling rapidly into the sky. That was that. It was the last ferry. The relief ship would go without Harmony. It would be four years before she could leave Earth.

In the same moment I felt exhilaration and dread. What she had done was marvellous and at the same time appalling. But my resolution was unshaken, and I knew by now it was unshakeable. I was going to find her, and tell her that whatever happened I would stay with her.

I went straight to look for Helix. And at least he was in his rooms. But the interview was a disappointment. Helix hadn't seen her. And he was not at all pleased when I told him of the message she'd left.

'I did all I could to make her see reason,' he said.

'But ... don't you think it's wonderful? To have such courage, I mean?'

'Foolhardiness. I wish she was on the ferry, Vector.'

'Well, she isn't. Do you know where she *is*?'

'I haven't seen her since yesterday evening, when you were here. I don't know anything about her movements since then.'

'Do you think she could actually have got outside?'

'I don't believe she could. The gate Guards are keen, and frightened of Dyne.'

'If I can find her,' I said, 'I shall go outside as well.'

Helix looked thoughtful at this. Then he said, 'At this stage, Vector, I won't discourage you. It might be the best thing. And now, if you'll excuse me, I must go and see Aria. She told me to wait until the relief ship had gone; and now it's gone.'

'It's about that business at the Survey Station?' I asked.

'Yes.'

'You think Dyne is getting too powerful, don't you, Helix?'

'Yes.'

56

'But Aria wouldn't listen when you tried to tell her about it before. Do you think she'll listen now?'

'Not really. But I have to try. Just as I have to try to keep juniors out of trouble.' He half-smiled, though he didn't look amused.

'Good luck, Vector,' he said. 'I hope you find her. She'll need a friend. And if you get outside, go and find the Community, in the East Quarter. See what they can do for you. You can tell them I sent you if you like – though they don't really approve of me.'

'Who are the Community? Why don't they approve of you?'

'You ask too many questions, Vector. The less you know about some things, the better for yourself.'

That was all I could get out of him. It wasn't the first time Helix had left me baffled. But speculation about Helix could wait. I wanted to find Harmony as quickly as possible.

I pondered the matter as I went out once more into the Precinct. Helix didn't think she could have got past the guardroom. There were no craft missing. She couldn't have escaped over the walls: not with that thirty-metre drop all round. It seemed she must be hiding somewhere. But what hiding-place could she have found?

Then the thought struck me. I strode rapidly across the Precinct, past the light-fountains and into the quiet area among the ornamental bushes. There was the seat where Harmony and I had sat so many times during the last few days. There too was the clump of greenery from behind which a Guard had spied on us.

I went up to it. No movement. Nobody to be seen. But then, it had concealed that Guard pretty effectively. And if it could conceal him, it could conceal someone else.

'It's all right,' I said. 'It's only me. There's no one else about.'

'Vector!' came Harmony's voice from behind the bushes. 'Vector!'

Chapter Six

'You're not safe there,' I said. 'They're still searching for you. And there must be at least one Guard who knows about that place – the one who hid in it himself.'

'I know,' she said. 'I'm waiting for Node.'

'Node?'

'Yes, Node. Don't hang around, Vector. Go back to your own Tower, please. This hasn't anything to do with you.'

'It has. If you're going outside, I'm coming with you.'

'But you said.... Oh, Vector, *please* go away, you'll only attract attention.'

That was true enough. I went away, but only as far as the light-fountain. There I stopped to consider. Harmony couldn't get outside without help, Helix had said, and she needed friends. She had always spoken of Node as a friend. How he could have become involved in this escapade I didn't know, but obviously he had. Unless he was on duty or was already on his way to Harmony's hiding-place, he was probably in his room in the Guards' barracks, beside the Bowling Green. And that wasn't far away.

There was still no sign that anyone was trailing me. I headed for the Bowling Green.

That was Guard territory. Strictly speaking, it was outside the Precinct, from which you reached it through a double gate which usually stood open. Like the Precinct itself, it was bounded by a high wall; and it had its own back gate into the outside world. The Green, from which the whole area took its name, was a square of smooth, flat, closely-trimmed grass, on which off-duty Guards often played a traditional Creature game. Arranged round the Green were the barrack-blocks in which the Guards lived, and also the health centre and the maintenance workshops. The general effect was neat, bleak and symmetrical.

There were several blocks, and I had no idea which was Node's. But I was barely through the gate when he stepped out of one of them and came briskly towards me. He was in uniform, wearing his Guard cap and carrying his greatcoat over an arm. He didn't look particularly pleased to see me.

'What are you doing here?' he demanded.

'Looking for you.'

'Why?'

'I've just seen Harmony,' I said. 'Among the bushes.'

Node looked round in all directions. Then his face creased into a cautious grin.

'You're not giving her away, are you?' he asked.

'No, of course not. I'm going with her.'

'That's good. That's great. But just now, things are difficult. Go to my room, Vector, quickly. It's E6. And stay there till I come.'

He hurried off. I moved rapidly towards the block I'd seen him emerge from. I knew well enough that a Person in the Guards' quarters was conspicuous. Luckily I passed only one Guard, who was sitting on the steps of a block polishing his boots and didn't even look up.

I mistook the number of Node's room, and peered first into a barrack-room that held some twenty beds. Each bed had its occupant's kit laid out on it neatly in a formal pattern, and a pair of boots shining beside it. Guards were always proud of their boots.

But that was E5. Node was in E6, and as a senior Guard he had a room to himself. It was small and bare, with a bed, a chair, a desk, and a wardrobe which stood open, displaying his spare uniform. The room also had a ceiling-speaker and wall-screen, a quickheat and a caller.

It took hardly any time to see what there was to see. I went to the window and, careful not to show myself, looked out over the Bowling Green. And there was Node, hatless, hurrying towards me, accompanied by a tall Guard in cap and greatcoat. They were out of my line of sight and in through the doorway of the block by the time I had corrected my first impression. No, it wasn't a tall Guard in cap and greatcoat. It was Harmony. A few seconds later they were in the room beside me.

I held my arms open. Harmony looked at me uncertainly at first, then came to me and I put them round her. Node was mopping his perspiring forehead.

'I didn't enjoy that at all,' he said. 'And we were only just in time. I could see from the corner of my eye as we came away, there was a pair of Guards heading for that end of the Precinct where you was hid, my dear. They'd have found you if you was still there, I don't doubt.'

'I shouldn't be letting you run such awful risks, Node,' Harmony said.

'It was me what offered to do it,' Node said; and then, to me, encouragingly, 'Go on, young Vector. Don't mind me. Kiss her properly, while I make you both a cup of herb tea.'

I kissed her properly.

'You really want to come outside with me, Vector?' she asked, when at length I'd released her and we were sipping the herb tea, which tasted abominable.

'Yes. Definitely.'

'You understand what that means, don't you? You heard Helix say that Creatures are usually hungry. You know they get diseases and don't recover, because they haven't any doctors. And everyone says that although Creatures are fairly harmless in the day-time they get violent after dark. That's right, isn't it, Node? I've heard you say you wouldn't risk being out by yourself in those city streets at night, and you're pretty tough.'

'Yes, well,' Node said, 'us Guards don't go outside except on patrol, you know. It don't make you popular, being a Guard. They'd tear us to pieces, some of them would, if they got the chance. I can't say I'm a Creature-lover myself. I wouldn't've encouraged you, when you came to see me last night, if I hadn't felt things was a bit out of joint in the Precinct just now.'

'What do you mean by that, Node?' I asked, but Node ignored the interruption.

'Mind you,' he said, 'it could be different out there for Persons from what it is for Guards. The Creatures don't see much of

Persons, except when the Regent makes an appearance. And they do have a kind of reverence for the Regent. So you might be all right, and then again you might not. There's no telling with Creatures.'

'You see, Vector, what kind of risk you're proposing to run,' Harmony said. 'Are you *quite* sure you want to do it?'

'Yes,' I said; and to my own surprise I didn't feel a moment's wavering in my resolution.

'Then you're as crazy as I am,' Harmony said. For the first time that morning she smiled. 'You know what, Vector?' And she added, in the earthy Creature phrase for which we had no equivalent, 'I love you.'

'I love you, too,' I said. 'We'll survive. We might even find Melody.'

'We got to get you away from here first,' said Node. 'And that's easier said than done.'

'Suppose you were on duty at the guardroom, Node,' said Harmony. 'Could you turn a blind eye as we slip out?'

'Oh, no, Miss!' Node declared with emphasis. 'It's not just me. There's three under-Guards on duty at the same time, and they'd all have to be persuaded. And I can tell you, they won't risk being sacked for letting someone go out that shouldn't. Have you ever thought what happens to a Guard that loses his job? He's thrown out into the city. No uniform, no barracks, no mess-room, no privileges. He's just a Creature, like thousands of others. You can't expect them to take that chance.'

'It's what you're risking now, Node, isn't it?' Harmony said.

'Never mind that. Just let me think. There's the back gate that goes out from behind the Bowling Green, of course, but that's locked at night and even more closely guarded in the day-time than the other, being under the eye of Dyne as you might say, his apartment being close by. So your best chance is to get past the guardroom. Now, let's consider, who *could* get past that guard-room? Adult Persons, of course, but you wouldn't pass for adults, not yet, and anyway they'd be looking out for you. Other Guards; but they know all the other Guards, so that's no use.'

Node paused, looking thoughtful, then went on:

'That only leaves Creatures. Now there's Creatures that live outside but are licensed to come in here to work. If I'd time I might fake you a permit, but that takes a bit of organizing. And then there's one last category. There's Creatures that sneaks in and out without permits. Thieving, maybe, or having some relative or friend among the servants that gives them food and things to take outside. Now suppose we was to disguise you two as a couple of Creatures. . . .'

'Disguise *us*? As *Creatures*?' I was appalled. 'You're going too far, Node. There *is* a limit. Anyway, a Person couldn't be mistaken for a Creature. That's absurd.'

'Oh, I don't know,' said Harmony. 'If we were dirty and ragged enough. . . .'

I was speechless, but Node nodded his head and grinned. 'That's right, Miss!' he said. 'You and Mr Vector, you ain't all that tall. You'll get by. Now if it was Mr Helix, the size he is, there'd be no concealing *him*!'

Node was looking pleased with himself now. 'I got it all worked out,' he said. 'We'll have you away from here on the garbage craft. Dawn tomorrow, that goes out. Leave it to me. But not a word to anyone about it, remember, as long as you live. You promise me?'

'It's a promise, Node dear,' said Harmony, and kissed him. I looked away.

Then the caller bleeped. Node answered it. I saw him grimace, then grin. After a minute or so, he flicked it off, turned to us and said, 'Dyne still wants you stopped, if you haven't got out already. He's put me in charge of the search.'

I was alarmed, but Node grinned again. 'Best thing that could have happened,' he said. 'With me organizing the search, I reckon you're in the safest place of all. Nobody's going to look for you here. This afternoon I'll report that you can't be found and I reckon you must have got away somehow. And tomorrow morning we'll get you out in reality!'

It was still dark when we arrived, unnoticed, at the garbage depot. Node led us to where the big, clumsy land-craft was parked. 'And this here,' he said, 'is Bert.'

Bert grunted. He was a swarthy Creature wearing a greasy, flat cap and overalls.

'Bert is a licensed Creature what drives the garbage craft,' said Node. He spoke a few words to Bert in what appeared to be a dialect of Creature, though to me it was almost incomprehensible. Bert answered him doubtfully in the same tongue. There were further exchanges. Then Bert held out his hand. Node put coins into it.

Money! Earlier, ignoring our protests, Node had thrust handfuls of coins upon Harmony and me, saying he had nothing on which to spend his pay. It was the first time I'd handled money in my life. I'd heard of it, of course. It was a primitive device used in the city, and in transactions between the city and the Colony, so that Creatures could be rewarded for their labours without the need for shunting actual goods around, and so that they could bargain among themselves. We Persons didn't use such a time-wasting system; we just took what we needed from the appropriate store. That was much simpler.

Node turned to us.

'It won't be so bad for you, Harmony,' he said. (I noticed that he'd dropped the 'Miss'.) 'You can sit beside Bert, up front. The gate Guards are used to Bert having a mate with him. They won't ask no questions. But you're out of luck, Vector. You'll have to go inside. And they might just cast a glance into the back. So you better get right down into the garbage and cover yourself up.'

'Ugh!' I was ready to retch. Already I was feeling itchy, grimy and a bit dispirited. I hadn't enjoyed the night spent on the hard floor of Node's room in the barracks, the changing into Creature rags which Node insisted were clean but which didn't look or feel it, or our furtive before-dawn slinking to the garbage depot, a smelly underside to the elegant Precinct which I hadn't even known to exist.

Harmony climbed into the front of the craft. She was wearing overalls like Bert's, and her cloud of hair had been squashed out of sight under her cap. Her face was smeared with dirt. She was strangely unrecognizable; it was almost as if some actual Creature had appeared in her place. She carried a haversack containing spare clothes – no better than those we were wearing – and an emergency ration of food concentrate.

Node was waiting for me to board the craft.

'When will we see you again?' I asked him.

'That's as may be,' he said. 'Don't count on it at all. But whatever happens, remember old Node did his best for you, eh? And look after *her*.'

He put out his hand. Recalling a practice I'd observed among Guards, I stretched mine out also and shook it. It was the closest physical contact I'd ever had with a Creature up to that time. Node's hand was warm and dry: not repulsive, as I'd expected. Then, reluctantly, I crawled into the back of the craft. It was an old-fashioned affair with a row of great grinding metal teeth, now mercifully at rest. I squeezed past them and covered myself with the stinking refuse.

Node shouted a farewell. The engine started, and the craft vibrated under me. Then, slowly, it rolled forward over the floor of the depot and up the slope that led out into the Precinct. Still moving slowly, it travelled a few metres, turned a corner, moved forward again and came to a halt.

It couldn't be at the guardroom yet. I waited. Two or three minutes passed. The touch and smell of the garbage were becoming intolerable; I resisted an almost overwhelming need to throw up. Then I heard the tail-gate creak, and there was a rustling and a sound of breathing inside the craft.

I half sat up and peered as best I could through the rubbish. There was very little light, but I knew at once what had happened. A Creature had crept into the craft, and was making its way as far inside as possible. This brought it in my direction. Almost at once it became aware of me. We stared at each other in the gloom. Then the Creature muttered something and began to bury itself in the refuse, close beside me.

The craft moved forward again. There was another brief halt, during which nothing happened that I could perceive. Then the slow crawl forward once more. And then there were voices all round, and I knew we had reached the guardroom. My sense of panic was now stronger than my disgust. I lay silently, conscious of the breathing of the Creature close beside me.

A Guard was shouting at the driver, in the harsh commanding tone which Guards always used to Creatures. I heard two or three responses from Bert, then more questions in different voices. Another reply from Bert, followed by silence. I waited on edge for the craft to move forward again; but it didn't. Two or three endless-seeming minutes went by. My heart thumped. This delay was lasting too long. Then there was a tramping of Guards' boots, the back of the craft slid up, and lights were shone inside. A heavy thud caused the craft to bounce on its springs and showed that a Guard had leaped on board.

'How many's there supposed to be, Root?' he bawled from close beside me.

'Only one,' came the answer from outside. And a moment later the voice which gave it continued, 'Broke into the clothing store, some time since midnight.'

So it wasn't Harmony and I who were being hunted. I had barely time to take this in before I felt a wiry grip on my arm and was dragged to my feet.

'Well, there's two here!' the Guard called. And the Creature and I were sent staggering towards the tail of the craft. Two more Guards grabbed us from the ground, forcing us to jump. The Creature hit one of them, broke free and began to run, but the first Guard had also jumped down from the truck and caught it almost at once.

The Creature and I were made to stand side by side with our backs to the guardroom wall. The Guard who had been hit buffeted the Creature hard on each cheek in turn. Then he turned to me, and I too received a couple of stinging blows.

'We take 'em inside, Root?' the first Guard asked.

'No. Keep them here for now. There's light enough to see what I want to see.' Root, who was clearly the Guard in charge, shone his light into the Creature's eyes.

'Quite a strong-looking brute, aren't you?' he said. He hit it in the face again. 'Raiding the clothing store, eh? Where's the loot? Save trouble and tell us now.' Another blow, which made the Creature's head jerk.

'He's wearing it!' said the first Guard. 'Or some of it!'

'So he is!'

The second Guard ripped the tattered jacket from the Creature's back. Under it he was wearing a new-looking Guard-style tunic, and below that there seemed to be more items of new clothing.

'So!' said the Guard in charge. 'You're going to have some explaining to do, aren't you?' He gave the Creature a further cuff, then turned his attention to me.

'What's this one got?' he inquired.

The Creature spoke up. 'Nothing to do with 'im,' it said. 'It was only me that did this job.'

'Covering up, eh?' said the first Guard, and added sarcastically, 'Noble, aren't you?'

'I tell you, I done it all myself,' said the Creature. Root hit it again. The first Guard was already tearing my clothing apart.

'Don't seem to be anything here,' he said.

'I keep telling you. . . .' the Creature began, but got another cuff for its pains.

'*You* haven't much to say for yourself, have you?' the Guard in charge remarked to me. I didn't answer. I was astonished that they hadn't instantly discovered that I was a Person – could it be that clothing made so much difference? – but was sure that if I spoke my voice would give me away.

And now the first Guard found the one and only sound pocket in the clothes I was wearing. He drew out his hand, holding the coins which Node had given me. The two other Guards craned to see them. Obviously they were quite valuable, for the Guards seemed impressed and exchanged meaningful looks. One of them said, 'No theft of money reported, is there?'

'No.'

'Where d'you get this from, feller?' the first one asked. I still stayed silent.

The Guard in charge said, 'Never mind where he got it from. We'll take care of it, eh? Let him go, now. Boot him out. We don't know nothing about it.'

The second Guard grinned. 'You're in luck, feller,' he said to me. 'Bought your freedom, as you might say. Not like the other poor sod. Now, get out of here, quick. See that door beside the main gate? I want you out through there before your feet touch the ground!'

I didn't wait to be told twice. I ran.

Chapter Seven

Nobody was pursuing me. After a few metres I slackened pace and stood, breathing the outside air in great gulps and feeling it cold and damp in my lungs. A line of perhaps a hundred Creatures, dimly visible in the grey dawn light, stretched downhill from the main gate. They swung their arms, stamped their feet and drew their rags closely round them. Many coughed and wheezed. Few spoke.

Node had disguised me well. Though taller than most of the Creatures in the line, I didn't attract any attention. No Creature of course would have expected to see a Person or Guard out here in such wretched dress. I joined the end of the line, since I wanted to keep the gate in view and this seemed the least conspicuous way of doing so. I was worried of course in case the discovery of stowaways in the garbage craft might cause the craft itself to be detained and questions asked of Bert and his supposed mate.

The Creature next to me wore a flat cap and had black bristles on its face. It grunted some kind of greeting.

'What's the line for?' I asked.

'Job line,' the Creature said, looking surprised. And I realized I should have known. This was the queue for casual work in the Precinct. Those who came early enough had a good chance of employment for the day, and possibly a meal thrown in.

Having taken so much trouble to get out of the Precinct, I hadn't the least wish to get back in, but there seemed no danger of that at present; the gates were closed and the line wasn't moving. More Creatures arrived and tagged on at the end; slowly the line stretched farther down the hill.

'We're too late, likely,' said a short Creature a couple of places away. 'They might run out of jobs before they get this far.' It looked speculatively at me. '*You'll* be all right, though. They pick the big ones out.'

Another Creature produced a small amount of some shredded material, which it rolled up in a bit of thin, white sheeting similar to the leaves of the Book. Inquiry along the line brought out a rough-looking firemaker, with which the Creature set light to the cylinder it had just made. It was then passed from hand to hand, each Creature in turn sucking in the smoke with evident enjoyment. I took my turn at this procedure, drawing in as little smoke as possible and nevertheless choking slightly on the acrid fumes.

Luckily, any attention I might have attracted was drawn away as the great transparent doors of the airlock slid aside. The Creatures stood straighter and the line tightened itself up as if for business; but all that actually happened was the emergence of the garbage craft. It trundled past most of the line, and stopped near the end of it.

Several Creatures broke ranks and gathered round the tail of the craft. But I was watching the front. To my relief the shapeless, dingy, flat-capped figure that I knew to be Harmony got out at one side. She was about to make off, but the driver went after her and grabbed her by the sleeve. I couldn't hear what he said, but when he held out a hand the meaning was plain enough.

Harmony rummaged in her clothing. There were shouts from the Creatures clustering round the back of the craft, and the driver answered them in surly tones. Harmony produced a couple of coins. The driver didn't look satisfied, but let her go. He opened the back of the craft and took small coins from several Creatures whom he then allowed to forage in the truck.

I didn't wait to see what they were finding there; it could only be garbage anyway. I followed Harmony, who had broken into a fast walk. We left the craft and the line of Creatures behind, and were soon moving downhill among the first shacks of the city.

I caught up with her and took her hand, but she pushed mine away.

'Drop back a bit,' she said.

'From what Aria said, it didn't sound as if they'd send out a search party,' I told her.

'We'd better not take any chances. Let's get as far as we can from the gate, quickly, and try not to be noticed.'

She stalked ahead. I fell behind, keeping her in sight but trying not to look as if there was any connection between us. The light was increasing now, and the city was coming to life. There were a good many Creatures about, all on foot; the only craft to be seen were a few handcarts.

After the first rash of shanties, the dwellings were more solid than I had expected, constructed from some kind of small, red building-block, though now dirty and dilapidated. They had window spaces but few windows, and there were curious devices on the roof-tops through which smoke emerged. Creature children, naked or scantily dressed, peered from doorways.

It was easy to tell male Creatures from females; their physical differences were like ours but more marked. Most Creatures were skinny; a few, mainly females, were fat but looked no healthier than the thin ones. Indeed, few Creatures appeared to be both whole and healthy. The proportion with deformities was high. Stoops, round shoulders and knock knees were among the least of these; there were crooked Creatures, Creatures with misshapen or missing limbs, Creatures marked by the ravages of diseases I could not have named.

They didn't seem threatening, though. I saw no violence that morning, except between children squabbling over scraps. No Creature accosted either of us. They appeared gentle and (considering their condition) surprisingly cheerful; they talked to each other and even sang in a tuneless way. I noticed that young males and females often walked with arms round each other and showed open affection.

Creatures seemed to spend a lot of their time standing in line. There were communal stand-pipes at intervals, from which they drew water, and there were stalls at which they waited to buy food: sometimes recognizable vegetables, other times unappetizing odds and ends which I suspected to be of animal origin. It was noticeable that the stallholders were better dressed than their customers, and almost invariably had strong, shiny, Guard-type boots. I discovered later that they were usually related to Guards and enjoyed some degree of Guard protection. Uncollected rubbish and ordure festered in the streets; the stench at first was sickening, but to some extent I quickly became acclimatized to it.

When we'd traversed three or four streets, Harmony stopped and waited for me to catch up. Behind the dirt stains there was distress in her face.

'I should think we're pretty safe now,' she said. 'But, oh! Do you wonder we're not allowed to see all this? How could we let it happen?'

'It's not very nice,' I admitted. 'I suppose even Creatures should be well fed and healthy.'

'*Even* Creatures?'

'Well, I know you keep telling me they're like us,' I said, 'but honestly, Harmony....'

'You can't accept it?'

'Not yet,' I said. 'Not quite.' But even as I spoke I realized that willy-nilly I'd gone a long way towards accepting it. It was the similarity of Creatures to ourselves that made their deformities so horrifying. I had never seen a deformed Person.

And yet ... my thoughts slid away to the Towers, and the cleanliness and delicate skins of Persons, and I thought of the colonists settling down to the Game or to a morning of music-making or pure mathematics; and although I'd hardly been out of the Precinct an hour I couldn't help wishing for a moment that I were safely back in there and away from these stinking streets.

'We may,' Harmony said, 'be here for the rest of our lives.'

That was something I couldn't believe. But I didn't want to argue with Harmony; I didn't even want to discuss the possibility. I said nothing.

'Anyway, I suppose we may as well look for those people Helix told you about,' she went on. 'Who knows? – they might even be able to lead us to Melody.'

'Yes, it would be nice to find them. I could do with a bath.'

'Who says you'll be able to have a bath?'

Then Harmony looked into my downcast face and smiled.

'Cheer up, Vector dear,' she said. 'We're alive and together and outside and free and breathing the air, and isn't it marvellous?'

She kissed me. The extraordinary feelings of the last few days came flooding back.

'I love you,' I said out loud in the old Creature phrase. An elderly Creature which was hobbling past turned round and grinned at us.

'And you're *not* going back, Vector. You're not having that operation.'

'No.'

'Try and look a bit more confident about it,' she advised me. And then, 'Shall I tell you something? I'm hungry.'

'So am I,' I said. 'Let's have some of our rations.'

'Shouldn't we keep them for an emergency?'

'Maybe. But what do we do now?'

'We buy something. We give money to one of these stallkeepers and get food in exchange.'

I told her how the gate Guards had taken my money.

'I still have mine,' Harmony said. 'I gave the small coins to the garbage-craft driver. But I kept the big ones.'

She groped in her overalls and brought out four or five large coins of some bright metal, which she handed to me. We pored over them. Almost at once a little cluster of Creature children collected around us, then a trio of adults: two males and a female. It seemed to be the coins that drew them rather than our appearance, which until then hadn't attracted any attention.

'You're lucky, ain't you, mate?' said one of the males to me. 'Where'd you get that?'

'He's got the money *and* the girl,' said the other. 'Not bad, eh? *I* saw her kiss him.' Both males looked at Harmony appreciatively.

'We want to buy food,' she said.

'Nothing to stop you, love, is there?' said the female. 'That'll buy plenty. Feed a family for a week on that, you could.'

The first male was still studying Harmony. 'You don't come from round here,' he said. 'You're not like us, not quite. Is she, Joe? She's not like us.'

Joe joined in the scrutiny. 'No, Bill,' he reported. 'She don't look like us. Don't sound like us, either. She's all right, though, isn't she? I could quite fancy her.'

I glared.

'You know what?' said Bill. 'I reckon she's one of *them*.' He made a gesture in the direction of the Precinct. 'And he's another.'

72

'I guess that's right,' Joe agreed. 'You are, aren't you, Miss?' And then, 'What you doing out here, dressed like that?'

'Sssh! Don't pester the young lady!' urged the female.

Several more Creatures had now gathered round. Most of their faces showed only puzzlement and interest, though I noticed that a tall, lean male on the fringe scowled and spat on the ground.

'They're Persons!' a child shrilled. Three or four other children picked up the cry, and the word passed from mouth to mouth among the adults: 'Persons!'

'We've left the Precinct now,' Harmony said.

The baffled expressions remained. I had the impression that the Creatures would have liked to ask questions, but that now they knew we came from the Colony they hesitated to do so.

'And we're hungry!' I added.

The circle opened up in the direction of a little row of stalls. All the Creatures watched with interest as we went up to the nearest of them, kept by a large female with a heavy face and small eyes.

Harmony and I hesitated over what to buy. There were rough-looking root and leaf vegetables: not the kind we were used to, but (if Helix was right) quite edible and nourishing. We didn't fancy them, all the same.

Several of the Creatures were pointing to a group of small clay dishes at the edge of the stall, each containing a piece of some light-coloured fibrous material.

'That's good stuff,' said Joe. 'Go on, you can afford it, you got lots of money.'

'Fresh today,' said the woman at the stall.

'What is it?' I asked.

'Cooked rabbit.'

I knew what 'cooked' meant; it was a kind of instant heat treatment applied to the foods that were used in the Guards' messes. But 'rabbit' was meaningless both to Harmony and myself; it wasn't part of the Creature vocabulary we'd acquired.

I looked doubtfully at the stuff.

'How much money?' Harmony asked, holding out one of the big bright coins.

'Twenty-two,' said the woman. But from the Creatures all round the stall there were cries of 'No!' and 'Don't pay it!'

73

'Twelve!' said one of the males.

'Ten!' piped up a Creature child.

There was a general argument in which neither of us took any part. The woman settled for fifteen of whatever units the coin represented. Harmony handed it over, and several pairs of Creature eyes watched closely as the stallkeeper counted out small, duller coins in exchange. Then Harmony and I were each in possession of a little clay dish of rabbit, whatever that might be. All the Creatures watched with interest as we tasted it. It had a strange, strong flavour, unlike that of anything I'd ever eaten. For a moment I was doubtful about it; then I decided it was highly palatable.

'All right, eh?' said a Creature.

'Very good indeed,' said Harmony.

We ate most of the rabbit. Harmony gave small pieces to three or four Creature children, who ate them appreciatively with loud, sucking noises.

'Rabbit,' I said thoughtfully. 'What *is* it?'

One of the Creatures took a stick and drew a picture in the dirt of an animal with long ears. We recognized it then, from our brief studies of Earth flora and fauna.

'Ugh! *Animal*!' I exclaimed. 'We've eaten dead animal!' And I almost threw up on the spot. Harmony looked queasy, too.

'Yes, yes, animal!' the female Creature echoed. 'Folk keep 'em in the backyard, if they got a backyard. Grow quick, breed easy. Good food.'

'That's right, Liz,' the stallkeeper said; and, to me, 'Have some more, dear.' But now that we knew what it was, neither Harmony nor I wanted any more rabbit.

The day was warming up, and the early mist had given way to sunshine.

'Let's be getting on our way,' Harmony said. We asked the Creatures about the Community, but without result. Most of them had no idea what a community might be, and none of them knew anything about this particular Community. They knew where the East Quarter was, however, and sent us on in the direction we were already taking.

A group of children walked, ran or danced along the street with us, gabbling to each other and darting up with great daring to touch us from time to time. Harmony tried to ask questions, but the children she spoke to giggled and ran away, returning to accompany us again at a safe distance. They appeared better nourished than their elders and showed fewer signs of ill-health; I wondered at what stage deterioration set in.

But I wasn't in a frame of mind for speculation. I was beginning to feel unwell, and the sensation increased rapidly. I tried to conceal it, but swayed. Harmony took my arm.

'What's the matter? Is it the rabbit?' she asked.

'No, it's a headachy kind of thing. The bright light and the change of temperature, I think. It's getting warmer all the time. And the smell doesn't help.'

'The rich air could have something to do with it, too,' Harmony said. 'I feel rather the same way myself. We'd better rest.'

We hadn't yet seen seats of any kind in the city, but we'd seen Creatures squatting on the ground or sitting on doorsteps. We didn't think we could sit on somebody's doorstep, and we didn't like the filth on the ground, but we found a relatively clean stretch of sidewalk and sat with our backs to a wall. The little group of children, quieter now, stood round in a semicircle, watching us from a respectful distance with great, wide eyes.

'I could do with a drink,' I said.

'So could I.'

'We could ask for water. They seem to be quite helpful.'

'But do you like the idea of drinking the water here?'

'Well, no.'

'They were selling drinks at one of those stalls,' I said. 'Coloured stuff. I saw a Creature drinking some. It seemed to like it.'

'It,' said Harmony. 'It. It. It. I wish you'd stop referring to them as "it". Please, Vector, can't you say "he" or "she"? The difference is plain enough.'

'I'll try,' I said. And from that time I don't think I ever again referred to a Creature as 'it', though it was quite some time before I realized the difference this made to the way I looked at them. 'But I *would* like a drink.'

'I don't think we should risk the coloured stuff. But there was fruit on that other stall. None of it very juicy-looking, but better than nothing. It might quench your thirst a bit.'

'There were some of those little things we call "plums",' I said.

' "Plums" is a Creature word, actually,' Harmony told me. 'We borrowed it. Well, the plums should be safe. I'll buy some. Now, where did I put that money?'

She felt in the pocket of her overalls, then searched all through her clothes. Then she looked at me in consternation.

'It's gone!' she exclaimed.

'You must have dropped it.'

'I don't think I did.' But she got up and searched the ground around us. I meant to get up too, but was feeling dizzy and decidedly ill by now. I half-rose, then sank back to the pavement.

One of the Creature children advanced.

'What you lost?' it inquired.

'I lost the money,' Harmony said.

'You lost all that money? That's bad!' the child said. The group gabbled together excitedly. Three or four of them began moving slowly up the hill, the way we'd come, searching all the way. Another ran ahead of them. And a minute later the three adult Creatures came hurrying down.

'You lost your money?' said Joe. 'That was quick. You've not had much time to lose it in.'

'Nor much space, neither,' said Liz.

One of the children piped up with a name.

'Sid!' it said.

'Sid! Sid!' Two or three others repeated it.

'Where *is* Sid?' inquired Bill. 'He was here when they was eating the rabbit. I know. I saw him get a bit.'

Two or three children looked at each other and then, as if by silent consent, made off down an alley-way opposite. The remaining Creatures chattered together in indignant tones. After a minute or two the children reappeared. They were hauling along between them a small, skinny, almost naked male child, which protested and struggled all the way. Its fist was clenched. Joe tried to prise it open. The child bit him. Another child cuffed it, hard, and it gave up the struggle and began to bawl. Its opened fist disclosed Harmony's coins.

Joe extracted the coins and handed them over, beaming. Bill buffeted Sid twice, once on each cheek, then turned him round and sent him off with a kick to the backside. He ran away screaming.

'You was lucky,' Bill said. 'And the kids was smart, catching him before he'd hid the money.'

Harmony pocketed the bigger coins and, in some embarrassment, held out the smaller ones in the general direction of the children. They looked towards the adults as if for guidance.

'Go on, take it!' Liz said. One of the children gingerly took the money from Harmony's hand. They retreated a few metres and gathered round in a ring, apparently making some elaborate calculation.

'I'm sorry about that,' Liz said. 'Most of the kids is good. There's just a few like Sid. You got to allow for it. They don't have much.'

'No good telling the Patrol,' said Joe. 'They don't care. We have to deal with the kids ourselves.'

'And not only kids,' said Bill.

'Of course, the Patrol is all Guards,' said Joe. 'Keeping us quiet, that's what they're for. Doesn't matter what goes on, so long as it don't cause *them* any trouble.'

'Guards! They'll get what's in store for them one of these days!' said Bill. 'King Creature, come, that's what I say!'

'Ssssh!' hissed Liz. 'Don't talk about that!'

I had been hearing these exchanges as if from a great distance. I was still on the sidewalk, propped against the wall. I had closed my eyes against the sunlight, which was now intense; in the Precinct the light-conditioning would have softened its harshness. My head throbbed.

'Now I can buy those plums,' Harmony said. She went away with the Creatures, and a little later came back by herself carrying a bag of fruit. I ate a little of it. It didn't do much to quench my thirst.

'You don't look well at all,' Harmony said. 'We'd better get you into the shade.'

But I didn't want to stay.

'I'm feeling much better,' I lied. 'Let's get on our way and find this Community.'

'We're not in *such* a hurry.'

'Remember, Helix and Node both said the city was dangerous after dark,' I reminded her.

'I know they did. But these Creatures are so *harmless*, aren't they? Don't you think people in the Precinct exaggerate it all?'

'Well, maybe. But I'll be happier when we're there.'

Actually I was thinking less of any dangers than of my own physical state. I felt thoroughly ill by now. I had had enough of the city streets and wanted to arrive somewhere and collapse.

We walked on. Harmony kept my arm firmly linked with hers. Twice we inquired about the Community, but still found nobody who had heard of it. We had no difficulty in getting directions for the East Quarter. But after half an hour I could do no more.

'I'm sorry,' I said. 'This is it for the time being.'

We were still among the endless mean streets which seemed to characterize the city, and although it was now early autumn and the worst of the summer heat was over it was oppressively hot by the standards of the Precinct. Just across the street, an empty house had been boarded up. There, surely, was a doorstep we could freely sit on. I sank down on it with a sigh of relief. Harmony sat down beside me, put an arm round me and a cool hand on my hot forehead.

'Perhaps,' she said in a slow, reluctant voice, 'you should go back to the Precinct after all.'

'What?' I said. 'And be separated from you? After all this? Oh no, I'm not doing that!'

The vigour of my own voice astonished me. I didn't *feel* vigorous. But Harmony's nearness was a comfort. I closed my eyes. She stroked my forehead gently. The pain in my head eased a little, and exhaustion took over. After a while I fell asleep.

I don't know how long I slept. Once I woke briefly, saw that Harmony also was asleep, and dozed off again. When finally I woke, my head still ached and my throat was drier than ever, but the heat of the day was over, the sky cloudy and the light less bright.

No one had disturbed us. It seemed that to passers-by we were just a pair of grimy-faced beings in commonplace Creature dress; and there was obviously nothing remarkable about sitting on doorsteps. I was beginning indeed to doubt my own Personhood; to feel we had reached a plane of total unreality.

Unexpectedly someone came past and recognized us. It was the

78

stallkeeper who had sold us the cooked rabbit. Large and solid in her stout though dowdy clothing and sturdy boots, she had a bag slung over her arm and held tightly to her side.

'Time you was getting back to the Precinct,' she said.

'We're not going back to the Precinct.'

The woman halted briefly and stared at us. 'Time you was off the streets anyway,' she said, and clumped on her way.

Harmony rubbed her eyes. 'There *aren't* many people around,' she remarked.

And indeed there weren't. The formerly crowded street had emptied. Doors which had stood open were closed, and I noticed for the first time that the unglazed window-spaces in most of the houses were barred. Lights flickered from inside most of them. It was dusk.

Harmony stood beside me and put her hands on my shoulders. 'How are you now, Vector?' she asked.

'I'm fine,' I said. It wasn't true. I could hardly stand.

'I wish I knew where we were going,' she said; and then, 'Do you think this Community really exists?'

'If it doesn't, we're in trouble.'

A scrawny cat sprang from a windowsill and melted across the street, just visible in the gloom. I jumped.

'It's my fault,' she said softly. 'If it hadn't been for me, you'd never have done anything so silly.'

'It's not your fault. I wanted to come. And of *course* the Community exists. Helix wouldn't have invented it, would he?'

'I suppose not. But if we don't get to it tonight, what will we do?'

'We'll find somewhere to sleep,' I said, 'and look for it properly in the morning.'

'Vector, you're splendid.' She kissed me. Then she shivered. 'There's a coat in the bag,' she said. 'Node warned me about the changes of temperature out here.'

I opened the bag and took out a coat of coarse cloth and indeterminate colour. I put it round her shoulders.

'I don't like it here, do you?' she said, shivering again.

I didn't. The onset of darkness was troubling me. And I wasn't used to being out in the open; in the Precinct one was always under cover and guarded. Here I felt weak and vulnerable.

79

A figure went past us, walking briskly. I hailed it, intending to ask once more for directions. It heard me, half turned, but wouldn't stop. Then, when no more than twenty metres past, it suddenly turned face-about and, moving swiftly but silently, passed us again in the opposite direction. And instantly three figures raced towards us, pursuing it.

Their footsteps went past, then slowed and halted. A pause. I took Harmony's hand. We stood with our backs to the wall of the boarded-up house. Three Creatures loomed up and stood around us. It was a curious parallel to our encounter with three Creatures before buying food earlier in the day: curious but sinister.

There was the scratch of a primitive firemaker, then the flare of a torch. The three closed in. They were young full-grown males. The one with the torch held it so as to cast light on us; I could see little however of the faces of the three.

One of them whistled: a long whistle, extremely loud, amounting almost to a howl, on a rising and then a falling note. A second stepped forward and took an edge of Harmony's coat between finger and thumb.

'That's a nice coat you got there,' it said softly.

The third held the torch closer to Harmony's face.

'She's a nice girl,' it said. 'Aren't you, darling?'

'Are you lonely?' asked the first.

I moved forward. Without saying a word, the second Creature dug me sharply below the ribs with an elbow, winding me. The first one put its hands on Harmony's shoulders.

'Leave her alone!' I said.

'If I was you, feller,' said the one with the quiet voice, 'I'd get away from here, quick.'

I could think of only one thing to do. 'We are Persons,' I announced in a loud, clear voice.

All three laughed derisively.

'So are we. I'm the Regent,' said one.

And then the door of the house that adjoined the boarded-up one suddenly opened. A stout female figure burst out, holding some domestic object with which it belaboured the three males.

'Get away from here, you useless scum!' it yelled. A swipe across the shoulders made one of them howl. The three fell back in disorder. Next minute Harmony and I were being dragged into the house and the door was closed behind us.

Chapter Eight

We were in the main living-room of a Creature dwelling. It was cramped and stuffy. A pool of yellow light surrounded a lamp on a central table but left the corners of the room in darkness. In an opening in one wall was a small open fire. Three or four wooden boxes, a chair and a couple of mattresses took up most of the remaining space.

And the room seemed full of people, all staring at us. There was the woman who had let us in, thickset with brawny arms and still holding the cylindrical wooden object with which she'd routed the young males outside. There were also a small thin adult male, another male who seemed less than fully grown, and a couple of Creature children.

'Well, what do you make of this pair, Dad?' the woman inquired.

One of the children interjected, excitedly, 'It's them two I was telling you about, Mum! The two that had their money stole. They're Persons, from up at the Towers!'

'Get away with you!' said the half-grown male.

'They are! They are, truly!'

'King Creature, come!' the woman said. 'Is that so? Here, let's have a look at you!' And then, almost instantly, 'This lad's poorly!'

I was in fact on the point of collapse. My head throbbed. The woman put a grimy hand on my forehead; I tried not to shudder at the touch.

'Feverish!' she said.

'If they really are Persons, Mum,' said Dad, 'somebody better go up and tell them at the Gate. They'll send out a land-craft, I dare say.'

'He needs to lie down,' said Mum. And at that moment I slumped towards the ground. I was dimly aware of being caught and held by Dad and the younger male, and of hearing Harmony explain that we didn't want to go back to the Precinct. Then my head went into a final dizzy spin and I lost consciousness.

When I came round I was lying in the same room on one of the mattresses, with several layers of covering laid loosely over me. Most of the Creatures had disappeared from the room, and so had Harmony. My head ached, and my throat was drier than ever. I lay for a while with my eyes open, oddly reluctant to do or say anything. Two or three Creatures came and went, moving quietly; then someone knelt down beside me. It was the woman they'd called Mum. In the poor light I could see little except that her face and eyes were dark and there was a gap between her front teeth.

'You're awake, aren't you?' she asked.

I croaked a 'Yes', and then, 'Thirsty'.

'I'll see what I can do,' the woman said. 'Jim!' A Creature child appeared. 'Go and get some water, Jim. Not from that bucket that's straight from the street tap. Take it from the covered pitcher.'

When the child returned I heard the sound – suddenly the most delightful in the world – of water being poured; then the woman put some kind of cup into my hand.

'That's all right, it's boiled,' she said. 'Don't swallow it too fast.'

I drank it and felt a little better, though my head was still both painful and muzzy.

'Where's Harmony?' I asked.

'Har – mo – ny.' The woman repeated what were obviously strange syllables, slowly. 'Your friend. Or missis. Is she your missis? No, you're too young to have a missis. Girl-friend and boy-friend, that's what you are. I can tell.' She winked.

'You're not like most Persons, eh?' she went on. 'Persons is cold, they say, clever but cold. I wouldn't like to be one of them myself, no offence meant. Though, mind you, I do like to see the Regent when she comes out on the balcony at Kismus. So tall and stately, she is. . . .'

'Yes, yes,' I broke in, 'but where's Harmony?'

I hadn't intended it, but the sharpness of a Person dealing with an over-familiar Guard or servant must have crept into my voice. The woman drew back.

'She's all right. She's having a lie-down, too, in the other room. She's not ill like you are, but she needs it.'

I was relieved, having had a sudden ridiculous fear that Harmony might have vanished and I might be all on my own in this dark, stuffy place, surrounded by Creatures.

'Thank you,' I said. It was the first time in my life that I'd ever thanked a Creature. 'And thank you for saving us from those three outside.'

'Oh, *them*!' the woman said. 'I'm not afraid of them, or any like them. Poor, feeble things they are. If you show a bit of spirit, they'll run a mile. It's only the big gangs you need to worry about. So never mind thanking me, just lie back and take it easy. You'll be better by morning, I dare say.'

I slept fitfully most of that night, waking from time to time in the darkness with a sense of nightmare. Where all the Creature family were I didn't know, but somehow they had contrived to leave the room to me. It was getting light outside when I fell into a longer sleep, from which I was awakened by Harmony's hand on my forehead. The Creature woman was beside her. Between them they dragged me into a sitting position, and Mum put a basin into my hand containing a peculiar-looking mess, half solid, half liquid.

'Stew,' she said, smiling. 'Stew.' And seeing my doubtful expression Harmony added, 'Just try it. It's good.'

My throat was still dry. I tilted the bowl and drank some of the liquid. Like the cooked rabbit of the previous day, it was more palatable than I'd expected. I put all thoughts of its possible origins out of my mind and tried to eat a little of the solid stuff, but my throat seemed to have a great lump in it and the food wouldn't go down. I wasn't hungry anyway.

'Sorry,' I said. 'I can't eat any more.'

Mum shook her head regretfully. 'It's rough,' she admitted, 'but it's the best we have.'

'That's not the trouble,' I told her. I explained my difficulty in swallowing.

'I think you're still a bit feverish, too,' Harmony said. 'And you've been muttering in your sleep.'

Mum looked concerned. 'I reckon we ought to get you back to that Precinct,' she said.

'Oh, no!' I exclaimed. 'Certainly not!'

'Well, maybe you'll be better tomorrow. If not, we'll send for the Wise Woman.'

'The Wise Woman?'

'Yes. Em Briggs. Trouble is, she expects paying.'

Harmony and I exchanged glances, but asked no more questions. The two children had come quietly into the room and were eyeing the bowl which I'd put down.

'Can we finish the stew, Mum?' one of them asked eventually.

'You sure you don't want it?' Mum asked me; and when I shook my head again she said to the child,

'Oh, all right, then. No, you keep your hands out of the bowl. I'll share it out.' And with her rough, clawed fingers she took pieces of solid food from the bowl and gave them to each child in turn. When all was gone except a little remaining liquid, she offered the bowl to me again and I emptied it.

The children turned their attention to Harmony. They were still a little awed, but one of them went to her and gingerly put out a finger to touch her cheek. Harmony picked up the smaller one and went out of the room, leading the other by the hand.

'Not easy, keeping children fed,' the woman remarked.

'I'm sure it isn't,' I said. Then, 'What's your name?'

'My name's Vi. But they all call me Mum in this house. Dad does, too.'

'That's short for Mother, isn't it?'

She nodded. 'Why don't *you* call me Mum? You're only a boy really, aren't you, even if you *are* a Person?'

'Mum,' I said thoughtfully.

'That's right.' She smiled and took my hand. It felt rather good to call her Mum, even though she was a Creature, and a fat, ugly one with gap teeth at that.

'There, what's *your* name?' she asked.

'Vector.'

'I like that. There's a boy living near here whose name's Victor, but we call him Vic for short. How old are you, Vector?'

'Seventeen, in Earth years.'

'I thought you was about that,' she said. 'And do you have parents in the Precinct?'

'Yes, I suppose I do,' I said. Actually I had seen little more of my father and mother in the last couple of years than of any other adults in the Colony. When I was very small on Annulus, my mother had looked after me for a while, and had later taken me daily to and from the nursery, as Person mothers usually did. But I don't think she was particularly interested in me; that was not expected. My passing into education and training had been virtually the end of the relationship. Since we came to Earth, she and my father had put in an appearance from time to time at the weekly Family Hour, but this was a duty intermittently and reluctantly performed, and it would cease when I attained full Personhood. It hadn't even occurred to me to consult my parents when Harmony and I were wondering how to solve our problem.

'If you've really left the Precinct, you won't be seeing them.'

'No, I suppose not.'

'That must be hard. I'd hate to be separated from my children.'

'How many do you have?'

'Just the three you've seen. There was six more that died. But the ones I still have seem healthy, I'm glad to say.'

'How dreadful, losing six. I believe it's fifty years since a Person last died in childhood.'

'Oh well, that's another world,' said Mum philosophically; then, looking at me with a tender expression, 'I never spoke to a Person as much as this before. I must say, you strike me as almost human.'

'Almost human!' I was outraged, and drew myself up in protest; but as soon as I rose from the floor weakness overtook me and I sank back.

'There, there,' said Mum apologetically, 'I been talking to you too long. You just go back to sleep. I want you to be well by morning.'

She helped me to settle down in my uncomfortable bed. It seemed very little time before I was awake again, but in fact it was now night. There were noises of whooping, howling and whistling which at first intruded into my dreams, then woke me, though for a while I was uncertain whether I woke or slept. The lamp was alight, but turned down very low. Mum, Dad and Harmony were all in the room, and so was the half-grown male who looked – so far as I could judge in the poor light and my own uncertain state – to be a little younger than myself.

After some minutes of noise from the street outside there was a crash as if something heavy had hit the door; then there were shouts in chorus, close by. I could distinguish the name Ken. The voices settled into a chant:

'Come – out – Ken! Come – out – Ken!'

'You're not going, Ken! You hear me? You're not going!'

'All right, Mum, all right!' the boy said.

The chant went on, more loudly: 'COME – OUT – KEN! COME – OUT – KEN!' There was a rattle as if stones were now being thrown at the door. Then a dirty, grimacing Creature face appeared at the barred window. The shock of it made me cry out. Mum turned to me.

'It's one of those gangs,' she said. 'Don't worry. They can't get in.'

The Creature outside gripped the bars of the window and tried to shake them, but they were firm.

'Get something and hit his fingers, Dad!' urged Mum. But Dad shook his head.

'I'm not asking for trouble,' he said; and then, to Ken, 'You'll have naught to do with them, tonight or any other night. You hear me?'

The Creature at the window let out a great shriek of raucous, derisive laughter.

'COME – OUT – KEN! COME – OUT – KEN!' it bawled. But out in the street the chant had ceased and the centre of disturbance had moved on. There were catcalls farther away, followed by jeers and counter-jeers as if a quarrel had broken out. Then a fresh outbreak of howling, a flurry of figures rushing past the window, a frenzied yell of pain.

'That's the other lot arriving!' Mum said. 'The downstreet mob. Oh well, if they have a fight it'll keep them all busy for a while. I just wish they could knock some sense into each other, that's all!'

But it was Ken's face that I was watching in the lamplight. He had the rapt expression of one who had heard an irresistibly fascinating call from far off. Mum and Dad saw it, too.

'You get to bed, Ken!' Dad told him grimly. 'We're keeping you in one piece, see. That door's locked, and you'll not get out without fighting me for the key!'

Ken said nothing, but flung himself, clothed, on the mattress at the other side of the room.

'G'night, lad,' Dad said to him in a softer voice; and then, 'Come on, Mum. Come on, Harmony. The gangs aren't going to bother us much tonight. We'd better let these two lads get some sleep.'

Mum bent down and pressed my hand. Then she and Dad withdrew, taking the lamp with them. Ken said nothing, but for a long time I had a sense that he was lying awake and radiating resentment. Then I was asleep myself; then it was morning – the start of my third day in the city – and my throat was still sore and my head still ached.

I was alone in the room; Ken, it seemed, was up and away. I tried to get to my feet, but all my limbs were weak, and I sank back. I must have made some sound, because a moment later the door opened and Harmony was beside me. She knelt down and kissed my forehead; a cool hand took mine.

'Vector, dear, you're so *hot*!' she exclaimed. 'I'm sure you still have a fever. I'll fetch Mum.'

Mum waddled into the room, peered at me shrewdly in the half-light, and placed her own hand on my brow, expunging Harmony's kiss which up to that instant I'd been able to feel on my forehead.

'Wise Woman for him!' she pronounced decisively; and then, to Harmony, 'You got some money, haven't you, dear?'

Harmony nodded.

'You have to give the Wise Woman something,' Mum went on. 'She'll be satisfied with fifty. Jim! Go and fetch Em Briggs!'

Once more Mum and Harmony tucked me back into bed. I dozed again. It seemed no time before the Wise Woman was there. She was a tall, gaunt Creature with dark, hollow eyes and a curiously resonant voice, in which the simple syllables of the Creature tongue sounded inappropriate. Her assistant, a gawky, round-faced girl with a large pouch slung over her shoulder, followed her into the room.

'First,' the Wise Woman said when she'd been told my symptoms, 'we must seek guidance. I need everyone in the house. The more seekers the better.'

Mum brought in Ken and the two children. 'Dad's still out looking for work,' she said.

'Then the rest of us must seek harder,' said the Wise Woman. She and her assistant, Mum and Ken and the two children all squatted on their haunches and joined hands. Mum drew Harmony into the ring. The Wise Woman gabbled a lengthy formula which echoed meaninglessly in my head but ended with the slow, solemn words: 'King Creature, guide my hand. King Creature, guide my eye. King Creature, come soon and make all well!'

'King Creature, come!' echoed Mum and the children. 'King Creature, come!' repeated the assistant after a brief interval. Then they all got up and the children ran heedlessly away.

'Now, does the lad have enemies?' the Wise Woman asked.

'He's a Person,' said Mum.

'I can see he's a Person, I'm not blind. Persons can have enemies.'

'Persons don't have enemies,' I said feebly. 'Enmity isn't Personlike.'

'Persons could have enemies they don't know of,' the Wise Woman said darkly. 'But there's no one that would be likely to cast a fever on you, eh, lad?'

'No, of course not.'

'Then it's risen from the ground,' the Wise Woman said. 'I shall send it back into the ground. Ella!'

The assistant came forward with the pouch.

'Spread the cloak, Ella!'

Ella took from the top of the pouch an expanse of rusty, black cloth and held it round the Wise Woman, forming a kind of tent. Under this cover the Wise Woman carried out some mysterious process involving other items from the pouch. She muttered incomprehensibly as she did so. The assistant's lips moved in unison with hers. Eventually, in response to a sharp instruction, Ella took the cloak away and began folding it back into the pouch. The Wise Woman turned towards us. She was holding a tiny cup.

'King Creature, put power into my potion!' she intoned.

'King Creature, put power into her potion,' said the assistant.

The Wise Woman put the cup to my lips. I resisted.

'Go on, swallow it, Vec!' Mum urged me. 'It'll make you better. Em knows what she's doing.'

'I know what the King Creature is doing,' the Wise Woman corrected her sternly. But at the same moment she winked at me and I guessed that her dramatic performance was meant to impress the audience. Behind it, I hoped, there was some medical knowledge.

I swallowed the draught, which was small and exceedingly nasty.

'That will work soon,' the Wise Woman said. She turned to Harmony. 'Your doctor in the Colony could do no better, my pretty lady,' she said. 'We Creatures have our little skills that you don't know of.'

'But you believe that fevers are cast by enemies?' Harmony asked.

'That's as may be,' the Wise Woman said. I thought there was the ghost of a smile on her face. 'I'm sure *you* don't have enemies, my dear.'

'I don't think so,' said Harmony. 'In fact I'm told Vector and I have friends in the city. Other Persons, I mean. The Community.'

'Oh, yes, the Community,' the Wise Woman said. 'I know the Community. And the Community knows me.'

'You know where they live?'

'Em knows everything,' said Mum admiringly.

'Your Ken knows, as well,' said the Wise Woman.

'I don't know nobody called Community,' said Ken.

'You know that big house in the East Quarter where Maggie and Tom and Candy and Tigger and Polly live.'

'Oh, *that*. Yes, 'course I know *that*.'

'That's the Community. Or rather, *they're* the Community. You could take these two there, couldn't you?'

'Sure. I'll take 'em any time,' said Ken.

'Would Vector be better in their care?' Harmony asked.

'He's all right here with Vi. By tomorrow he won't need care, he'll be well. Whether he'd be happier among his own kind I don't know.'

'I suppose we ought to find them anyway,' said Harmony.

This conversation was coming to me from an increasing

distance. The dose the Wise Woman had given me was having its effect. Sleep rose into my brain like fumes. For a little longer I could hear voices but not take in any meaning. Then I heard nothing. I didn't know when the Wise Woman left. I woke during the night to hear Ken breathing in the other corner of the room, but no sound came from the street. Then I woke and slept intermittently for a long time. And then once more it was morning, and apart from a slight weakness in the legs I felt perfectly well.

Harmony came in and kissed me, and I put an arm round her and felt full of love and hope. Mum gave us bowls of a thick, coarse-textured stuff that she called porridge.

'And today,' said Harmony when we'd eaten it, 'we'll go in search of the Community.'

Chapter Nine

Mum was sorry to see us go. She reached up to each of us in turn, with her short, fat arms outstretched. We both embraced her. The children, Jim and Sal, had to be kissed as well on their dirty faces.

'You're sure you're all right, Vec?' Mum asked. 'Shouldn't you stay another day and get stronger?'

There were tears in her eyes when I said we felt we had to leave.

'Sentimental old thing, ain't you?' said Ken to his mother; and, to me, 'She'd be the same about a stray animal!'

'Kenneth!' Mum protested, shocked. 'You can't compare Persons and animals!'

'I can compare anything I like,' said Ken, who sounded cheerful enough this morning, though he'd been up at dawn and failed to find work. He said he would rather take us to the Community house than hang around doing nothing.

Mum wouldn't accept any money from Harmony.

'I know it looks a lot, what you got there,' she said. 'Can't remember when I had that much myself. But it won't go far if you both have to live on it.'

Ken led us out into the street. The atmosphere was comfortable enough, and I realized that I was getting used both to the richness of the air and the smells of the city. The news of our being at Mum's house seemed to have got around among her neighbours; women lining up at street taps called greetings to us, and two or three small children ran alongside until Ken sent them on their way.

We were still going downhill, but the land levelled off before long. Streets became broader, and there were large buildings whose original purposes I couldn't guess. Most were now used for living in by large numbers of Creatures. Among them were the higher structures we knew as the Stumps, which were also full of people. Seeing the Stumps reminded me of the Towers; and, looking back, I could see them rising, clean and shining, into the morning sky. The Towers were beautiful, beautiful.... For a moment, once again, I wished myself back amid their peace and elegance, but I put the thought sternly out of mind.

Soon a broad street brought us to the river, which was slow-flowing and murky. Some Creatures appeared to be swimming or bathing in it; others were taking water from it in pails. Ken grimaced.

'Sooner them than me!' he said. 'No wonder their guts is the way they are.'

You could tell that at some time there had been four bridges across the river, and all had been destroyed. One of them remained in ruins; the row of piers that had supported it projected uselessly from the water and a couple of small boats were plying between the banks. The other three bridges had been repaired in a makeshift way.

'Musta been quite something in the good days, them bridges,' Ken remarked.

'Why aren't they rebuilt?' I asked.

'Who's going to rebuild them? We don't have the know-how no more. The bad days took that from us. Creatures knew a lot before the bad days came. Now we don't know nothing. Only you Persons know much, and you're not interested in us.' For a moment he sounded bitter.

'When did the bad days come?'

'Oh, years and years ago, I dunno exactly.'

We got little more information from him. It seemed that long ago there had been good days, when Creatures had plenty to eat and stout clothes to wear. Then there'd been quarrelling and fighting and huge numbers killed, and the bad days came and were still here. That was Creature history as known to Ken.

We crossed one of the bridges and headed into a fresh maze of streets. Ken seemed to know his way.

'We're in the East Quarter,' he told us. 'Not far now.'

He looked about him with increasing caution às we went on. 'I don't often come over here,' he remarked. 'Not many folks around, is there? There could be daylight gangs, for all I know. Keep your eyes open.'

'What do we do if anything happens?'

'Run.'

'Are there gangs in all areas?' Harmony asked him.

Ken nodded. 'Mostly night-time, though,' he said.

'Ken,' I said thoughtfully, 'when that mob was pounding down the street the other night I thought you looked ... interested.'

Ken was slightly shamefaced. 'Well,' he said, 'when it's day-time and I got something to do and somebody to talk to, like now, I don't want to have anything to do with that lot. But at night, cooped up indoors, when you hear them coming down the street, all the sound of it, it's – well, it's exciting, it does something to you, makes you want to be out there with them, makes you feel like they're alive and you aren't.... Understand?'

'Sort of,' I said. I tried to visualize a gang of Persons, but the idea was too wild to imagine.

We were moving into an area where a street pattern remained but most of the buildings seemed to have been destroyed. There were fragments of old walls here and there, and occasionally there were exposed cellars, into which it would have been all too easy to fall at night.

'Too much cover for my liking,' said Ken, still wary.

But there was no sign of trouble. We came eventually to a large, square building, approached through a gate and across a courtyard. A barefoot, drably-dressed female walked through the gate ahead of us, stooping under the weight of a couple of buckets which she'd just filled from a street tap.

Ken hailed her and she turned round.

'Hi, Maggie! I brought some folks to see you!'

'Oh, yes?' The woman looked cautiously at us. 'Why?'

She was ten or maybe fifteen Earth years older than Harmony or myself. Her face had been pale but was weather-browned, and she looked lean and healthy. She wore a cap that fitted closely to her skull. Though she was tall for a Creature, you wouldn't at first sight have thought there was anything odd about her. It was her eyes that gave her away. The irises were clear and almost colourless. Those were Person eyes.

Harmony said, speaking in Person, 'We've come from the Colony. We had to leave. You must belong to the Community we were told about before we came outside.'

The woman answered in Person, slowly, as if our tongue had grown strange to her, 'I didn't know we were famous in the Colony. I thought they'd written us off years ago as a few freaks who gave up civilized life.' She added in Creature, 'This is how we speak now.'

'That's better, Mag,' said Ken. 'Talk so's I can understand you. I can't make nothing of that other stuff.'

'Are the Guards after you?' Maggie asked us.

'I don't know,' I said. 'I hope not.'

Maggie called, 'Tom! Tom!'

A man emerged from an outbuilding. He was brown-faced and had the same tell-tale colourless eyes. He wore an apron.

'There's two young Persons here from the Colony,' Maggie said.

Tom studied us with interest. 'You wouldn't think so from the way they're dressed,' he said. 'Anyway, why don't we ask them in?'

'The Guards might be looking for them.'

'We can risk that for a few minutes, can't we?'

Maggie led the way reluctantly into the house. So far as I'd thought about the Community at all, I'd thought of it as inhabiting elegant, spacious, Personlike quarters. It was a shock to see that this house, though quite large, was as dingy, ill-lit and inadequately furnished as Mum's hovel.

'Let's all have something to drink,' Tom said. He drew off liquid from a container which simmered over a fire. The drink was one of those herbal infusions that always made me pull a face.

'Not for me, thanks,' said Ken decisively. 'I got to go now. Gimme a carrot instead.'

'All right, Ken,' said Tom. 'Pull one up from the patch on your way out. One, mind you, not two or three.'

'Trust me,' said Ken. 'So long, all.' In a minute he was gone.

'And now,' said Tom, 'what did you do?'

'I don't understand you,' I said.

'I mean, why did you have to leave the Colony?'

'We wanted to be together,' I said.

'And was that the only reason?' Maggie asked. She sounded as if she didn't think it a sufficient one.

'Well, there was another,' Harmony said. 'I'm looking for my sister, who went outside three or four years ago. Melody.'

Maggie flashed a quick look at Tom. He met her eyes for a moment. I had the impression they were both startled.

'You wouldn't by any chance know what became of her?' Harmony asked.

'We've never heard of her,' said Maggie sharply. And then, 'Why come to us?'

'Helix suggested we should,' I told her. 'He said we'd need friends outside, and mentioned you.'

'You hear that, Tom?' Maggie said. 'Helix sent them. And for all we know they may be dodging the Guards. I don't like the sound of it.'

'You see,' Tom said to us apologetically, 'we try not to attract the Guards' interest. In the Colony the Guards are there to serve the Persons. But out here they do as they please.'

'And the less we see of them the better,' Maggie added.

'What's more,' said Tom, 'our experience of people coming here from the Colony hasn't been too happy. First there was. . . .'

'Careful, Tom,' said Maggie.

'There was one who brought trouble on us and walked out,' Tom continued. 'And there was one who'd been ejected from the Colony for cheating at the Game. He joined the Community and cheated *us*, too. Did no work and expected us to support him.'

'What happened to him?' I asked.

'He died of a fever. And then there was – still is – the one who wouldn't have the operation and started getting involved with female servants.'

I was horrified. 'Involved with *Creatures*!' I cried. 'That's bestiality!'

'So they thought in the Colony,' said Tom. 'Out he went. And came to us. And is still here, unfortunately.'

'You talk too much, Tom,' said Maggie.

'I'm just explaining,' said Tom, 'why the arrival of two more Persons doesn't fill us with instant joy.'

'These two aren't joining us, are they?' said Maggie.

'We haven't *asked* to join you,' I said.

Tom seemed surprised. 'If you don't join us, how do you propose to survive?' he inquired.

I hesitated.

'That's their problem, not ours,' said Maggie.

'Now, now, Maggie,' said Tom. 'Don't be unwelcoming. I quite like the look of these two.'

'Would you *let* us stay?' Harmony asked.

'I can't say,' said Tom. 'We'd have to consult the others.'

'What can you do?' Maggie asked.

'Do?'

'This isn't the Colony, you know. We work for a living. What can you do that would help us make a living for seven instead of five? No work no eat; that's the rule here.'

'We don't really know how livings are made,' Harmony said.

'Maggie does carpentry,' said Tom. 'Candy weaves cloth. You'll see her loom in the outhouse. I mend shoes. Tigger's line is house repairs.'

'From what I've seen, there can't be much new cloth sold in the city,' I said. 'And most Creatures don't wear shoes.'

'Correct,' said Tom. 'And most houses don't get repaired. But we do what we can when we can. As for Polly, he doesn't have a trade. He works at a foodstall. We don't like it much; the stalls are all Guard-owned or Guard-protected; but it's a way of earning, and sometimes there are leftovers. And we all do a share in the house and garden. We live off our own produce a good deal.'

'We've renounced everything connected with the Colony,' said Maggie. 'Even our names. If you joined us, you'd do the same. I was called Madrigal once, and Tom was Tensor.'

'I'd almost forgotten it,' said Tom. He turned to us. 'What are *your* names?'

We told him.

'Harmony could be Hatty,' said Maggie thoughtfully. 'And what about Vector?'

'He could be Vic,' said Tom.

'And now,' said Maggie, 'to return to my question, what can you do? Play the Dimension Game, no doubt, and compose a sonata.' She sounded scornful. 'But what can you do that's useful?'

'I don't think I can do anything,' I said.

'I can read and write Creature,' said Harmony.

Maggie and Tom looked at each other.

'Marks-on-paper writing?' said Tom. 'That could have its uses. Creatures do need to have something written for them occasionally.'

'There's two or three scribes in business already,' said Maggie. 'But I dare say there's work for another.'

'Let's go and bring the others in for lunch,' Tom said to her. 'And we'll have a quiet word on the way. Hatty and Vic, you can wait here. We shan't be long.'

For a minute or two we were alone. I turned to Harmony. 'Do we really want to join them?' I asked. 'I don't like Maggie much.'

'We should stay here if we can,' Harmony said. 'They know something about Melody.'

'Maggie said they didn't.'

'I know. But I could tell from their faces. They soon covered up, but I'm sure there was something there.'

'I noticed it too,' I admitted. 'But there isn't only Melody to think about, there's ourselves. We came out of the Colony to be together – just us. You know what I mean.' I thought of the couples we'd seen walking around openly, arms round each other, and excitement stirred in me.

Harmony smiled. 'Don't worry, Vector,' she said. 'Our time will come.'

Then we heard voices outside. There was just a moment in which she could kiss me before they all came in.

'This is Candy, formerly Cantata,' Tom told us. 'And Tigger, who used to be Integer. And Polly, otherwise Polygon. I want you all to meet our guests, Hatty and Vic.'

The new arrivals gathered round us, curiously. Only their tallness and the colourless eyes would have told anyone they were not Creatures. Like Tom and Maggie, they were coarsely dressed, and their hair was hidden under close-fitting caps. Candy and Tigger were stringy; Polly however was well built and had, for a Person, an unusual amount of bounce and crude vitality. It took me about ten seconds to realize that he must be the Person who'd been thrown out of the Colony for misbehaviour, and another ten seconds to see that he was inspecting Harmony with great interest. I found I resented it intensely.

Maggie went across to the big, ugly cooking-device, stirred a great pot, and ladled something out into bowls. Tom brought the bowls across and put them on the scrubbed, wooden table. Everyone sat round it. I knew what the food would be. It was stew again, and mostly vegetable. But I was hungry after the three days of fever during which I'd eaten hardly anything. I swallowed the stuff with relish and accepted a refill.

Meanwhile Maggie and Tom were telling the others of our history. I noticed that neither of them mentioned Melody, and some instinct warned me not to do so myself.

'How interesting to be – what's the phrase? – in love,' observed Candy, whose face was a little rounder and softer than Maggie's. 'I can't say I've ever felt like that myself, and so far as I know nobody's ever felt like that about *me*. I'm just an ordinary Person, I guess; female, but not very. But I think I understand.' Her voice was wistful.

Maggie was less sympathetic. 'That's all very well,' she said, 'but we haven't time for that sort of thing here. And there's another point. We like a quiet life. Hatty and Vic seem to be friends of Helix. We don't want to ask for trouble.'

'You know Helix, then?' I inquired.

'Oh, yes, he came to see us once. Talking about Creature advancement and the need for change. Well, it's all right for him, sitting there in the Colony. He isn't vulnerable like we are.'

'Helix says attitudes have to be changed in the Colony itself,' said Harmony. 'He says this is the Creatures' planet, and sooner or later they'll have to take over.'

'Then he can do something about it himself,' said Maggie sourly. 'It's no good looking to *us*.'

'The Creatures have got to act on their own behalf,' said Tigger.

'But at present they're too frightened of the Guards to do much for themselves. They'd rather rely on the King Creature.'

'Oh, yes, the King Creature!' I said. 'What on earth is the King Creature?'

'It isn't anything really,' said Tom. 'The King Creature is just folklore. There's a popular belief that some time in the future, when things are at their worst, the King Creature will emerge and lead his people to triumph and prosperity. Hence the saying—'

'King Creature, come!' chanted everyone in chorus.

'He'll be a magnificent Creature, as tall as a Person but broader and stronger, with red hair and a flaming red beard. And, some say, a flaming sword in his hand,' Tom concluded.

'The trouble with belief in the King Creature,' said Tigger, 'is that it excuses the ordinary Creatures from actually doing anything. They think they can just sit and wait. And in reality, of course, the King Creature *won't* come. Sometimes I think that nothing will ever happen.'

'Don't be too sure,' said Polly. There was a mischievous note in his voice. 'There are rumours in the city. Some folk reckon the great day might be nearer than you think.'

'Tavern gossip,' snapped Maggie. 'Just the kind of thing you *would* come home with, Polly. I'll believe it when I see it. The rumour-mongers would do better to work than talk. Speaking of which, it's time we all got back to work.'

'What are we going to do about these two?' asked Tom.

'I suggest,' said Tigger, 'that they stay with us for a few days and try our way of life. Then, if they like us and we like them, they can join the Community.'

'And what's Vic going to contribute?' Maggie asked.

'He could look after the house and vegetable garden,' Tigger suggested. 'That would give us all more time for our own work.'

There were sounds of assent from the others. Maggie accepted the verdict.

'But listen,' she said, turning to us, 'this is not a love-nest, you understand. We're here to work. At night, the girls sleep in one room and the men in another, and that's that. No fooling around!'

'Oh, Maggie!' protested Candy.

'What's the "Oh, Maggie" for?' inquired Maggie coldly.

Candy blushed, then said, 'They're young, and ... fond of each other. Aren't we being a little harsh?'

'We have our rules. They should obey them,' Maggie said. 'Isn't that right, fellows?'

'I suppose so,' said Tom. 'There's a Creature saying, "When in Rome do as the Romans do."'

'What or where is Rome?' I asked.

'I haven't the slightest idea.'

'I hope Vic and Hatty will stay with us,' said Polly. 'I'm sure we shall all be very happy together.'

I looked at him suspiciously. I still didn't like the way he'd been eyeing Harmony. But his expression was innocent.

'Thank you all very much,' Harmony said. She and I exchanged glances, and both nodded.

'Yes,' I said. 'We'd like to give it a try. Let's see how we get on.'

'All right,' said Maggie. 'All right. But if the Guards come looking for you, you needn't think we're going to hide you.'

At that moment a loud and repeated knocking at the door began. Tom went to investigate. He was back within seconds.

'The Guards *have* come,' he said.

Chapter Ten

There would have been no time to hide, even if the Community members had been disposed to conceal us. Tom had hardly spoken when a pair of uniformed Guards came into the room. I didn't know either of them. They seemed to be of fairly low rank.

'Stay where you are, please,' one of them said. 'Who is in charge here?'

There were exchanges of glances between the members. Then Maggie stepped forward.

'We don't have anyone in charge,' she said. 'This is a group of equals. But you can speak to me if you like.'

'Very well, Ma'am,' said one of the Guards. He spoke respectfully, as if fully conscious that he was addressing a Person. 'I would like you to help us if you will. We are searching for somebody.'

There seemed no point in spinning out these proceedings.

'All right, Guard,' I said. 'We're here. And nobody has been harbouring us. We've only just arrived, in fact.'

The two Guards stared at each other.

'"We"?' said the second one. 'Who's "we"?'

'Harmony and Vector,' I said.

'We left the Colony three or four days ago,' Harmony added. 'We thought you must be looking for us. Aren't you?'

'Harmony,' said the first Guard to the second. 'That's the girl who jumped ship. Remember?'

'I remember,' the second Guard said. They still looked puzzled. 'And the boy's her friend who disappeared the same day, I suppose?'

'I guess so. But that search was called off. We don't have any instructions about them now, do we?'

'No. So what do we do?'

There were more sounds outside. Through the door, now open, strode a third Guard. I knew him slightly. He was a senior Guard called Span, with a narrow face, sharp eyes and thinning sandy hair. The first two Guards jumped to attention as he entered.

'Well? Any sign?' he demanded.

'No, Span. We haven't really inquired yet. But there's this pair here, who got out a few days ago.'

'Never mind them. What about Helix?'

I gasped. 'You're looking for *Helix*?' I asked, incredulously.

'Be quiet, you!' said Span.

The first guard addressed Maggie again. 'I must ask you, Madam,' he said, 'whether you are acquainted with a Person of the name just mentioned.'

'"Madam!"' echoed Span. There was irritation in his voice. 'Why "Madam"?'

'They *are* Persons, Span.'

'They're nothing out here,' Span said. 'They're dirt, same as Creatures. This is how much I care about them.' He advanced and slapped Maggie's cheek, then turned and did the same to Tom. Nobody moved a finger.

'Now, you!' he snapped at Maggie. 'I don't have to ask you if you know Helix. You know him perfectly well. Where is he?'

'I have no idea where Helix is,' said Maggie with dignity, though her cheek was scarlet from the slap; the skin of Persons marked easily. 'I haven't seen Helix for months.'

'He's not in this room, that's for sure,' said the first Guard.

'All right, then. Bring the others in. Do the place over.'

'You won't find him,' Tigger said. 'He isn't on the premises, I assure you.'

'Speak when you're spoken to,' Span told him. 'And stay right here. Don't move, any of you.'

Another half-dozen Guards appeared in the doorway. They were detailed to search the house and grounds. Over the next half-hour we heard them doing so. They weren't being gentle about it. Crashes and scrapings marked their progress. Span stayed in the room with us, watching us with those sharp eyes as if daring us to move a muscle. From time to time he fired a question at one or other member of the Community, but didn't get any information. Nobody admitted to any recent knowledge of Helix. To us alone Span said nothing.

At length the first Guard came back and reported. 'No trace, Span,' he said.

'All right. Prepare to move on. I'll see you outside.'

'There's some useful things around,' the Guard said. 'Can we . . . ?'

'Only what you can easily carry,' said Span.

'And what about these two?' asked the second Guard. 'They were being sought a few days ago.'

'That's old news,' said Span. 'They're written off now. No pursuit order in force. We'll report that we saw them, that's all.'

I couldn't restrain myself. 'What's Helix *done*?' I demanded.

For answer I got a blow to each side of my head in turn. 'Mind your own business!' Span told me. And, to the Community members at large, 'If Helix appears, you tell us right away and hold him till we come, understand? If you help him in any way. . . .' He left the threat unfinished.

A few minutes later the Guards were all gone. The Community members, not having been told they could move, stayed where they were for a while longer before going to inspect the damage.

'Not as bad as it might have been,' said Tom afterwards. A few items of already-battered furniture had been knocked about a bit, some small possessions had been taken, and Tigger announced ruefully that the rhubarb wine he'd been making had gone. The garden was trampled, and every carrot had vanished from the patch. Worst of all, some garden tools had disappeared.

'We can't replace those,' said Tom. 'A good job they didn't find the ones we hid under the sacks in the shed.' Then he glanced across at us.

'Well,' he said to Maggie, 'the Guards weren't interested in Hatty or Vic. Surely that removes any doubt about letting them stay.'

Maggie, who seemed to be in a state of shock, said nothing but nodded in agreement.

We stayed.

The next few days were frustrating, however. We didn't learn anything about Melody. Our questions to individual Community members were side-stepped or parried; it was clear that if they did know anything about her they had agreed not to tell. We were just as much in the dark about Helix, whom they also seemed reluctant to discuss. My own guess was that Aria had refused to listen to his warnings about Dyne, that he had walked out of the Colony in disgust, and that once he had left the safety of the Precinct a vengeful Dyne had set the Guards on him. But I wasn't entirely satisfied with this explanation. Helix was an experienced Person and would have known what risks he ran.

In any case, where was he now? The days went by, and we neither saw him nor heard any news.

For me, however, the worst frustration was that Harmony and I were hardly ever alone together. As Maggie had said, the Community wasn't a love-nest. Work began early for everyone, and continued with brief meal-breaks until mid-evening. Then came supper and a little quiet conversation, and then it was bedtime. Harmony slept in the women's room and I in the men's.

My work was hard. I had to clean the house, keep the big, clumsy stove going, tend the garden, look after the rabbits which the Community kept in a row of hutches, and do a great many odd jobs. And everything was done in laborious and time-consuming ways, without even the most primitive electronic equipment.

Maggie was inclined at first to find fault, but gradually mellowed. She had taken it on herself to introduce Harmony among the Creatures of the neighbourhood and make known her willingness to act as scribe. In the evening I would sometimes look over Harmony's shoulder as she sat at the candle writing letters, or applications for work, or records of pitifully small transactions. But if my hand or cheek touched hers I could be sure that a warning cluck would come from Maggie, who obviously saw such gestures as a threat to the smooth running of the Community. No one left the premises after dark; we were told firmly that it was dangerous to do so, and if Harmony and I went into another room together or wandered out into the garden, there would be Maggie, keeping her inevitable eye on us.

Harmony at least was able to talk to Creatures from time to time. I myself saw nobody from outside except a boy called Nick who came occasionally to collect vegetables for sale. But one Person with whom I did manage to converse was Polly. His work as helper at a foodstall started early and finished by mid-afternoon. Sometimes, I knew, he would go after work to Creature taverns and even less reputable places; other times, when he had no money, he would come home and talk to me as I worked in the house or garden.

He never offered to help, but would sit on the kitchen table dangling his legs, or if I was outside would sit on the upturned wheelbarrow. (This was a curious one-wheeled craft, used for pushing soil or garden refuse around.) Occasionally he would ask questions about what was going on in the Colony these days; more often he would regale me with long accounts of his sexual exploits, culminating in an affair he claimed to have had with Trill, the wife of Dyne.

'Persons turn up their noses at Creature women,' he said one day when he'd been at the tavern and was a little the worse for parsnip ale, 'but believe you me, some of them are not bad at all. Feeding makes a difference, naturally. The best fed ones are best.'

'I didn't know any Creatures were well fed,' I said.

'You don't know much, do you? The attractive ones are best fed because they've something to trade for their food. And the best fed ones are the most attractive. A beneficial circle, you might say. There's nothing like a nice, plump, juicy Creature woman, Vic. One of these days I'll take you out and introduce you to one. It'll do you good.'

He noticed my expression of disgust. 'Of course, I was forgetting,' he said. 'You have that rare being, an attractive female Person, at your disposal. You've no need to envy my little peccadilloes. I'll confess, in fact, that I'm rather envious of *you*. Hatty – or Harmony, as I admit I prefer to call her – is quite delicious. Worth being turned out of the Precinct for, I should think; eh, Vector?'

He winked at me. I flared up.

'Take your filthy mind off Harmony!' I told him. 'She's not "at my disposal", or anybody else's!'

'O-ho!' said Polly. 'You mean you haven't, you actually haven't, er...?'

'It's none of your business. But as a matter of fact I haven't.'

'I was sure I saw you kiss her the other morning.'

I blushed. 'Maybe you did. But that was affectionate, that was because I'm fond of her.'

'Yes, yes, my dear Vector. How young you are, how little you know of life. And how interesting that you haven't, er. . . .'

'You needn't think *you're* going to!' I cried.

'That would be for her to decide, wouldn't it?' said Polly.

I hit him on the cheek. He didn't stop smiling, though a red patch appeared on his face at once, and though all Persons are sensitive to anything that mars the appearance of their skin. He put his fingers to the place.

'That was unPersonlike, Vector,' he said chidingly. 'But I must admit you show spirit.' He got up from the wheelbarrow and wove an uncertain course towards the house.

'You shouldn't have done it,' Harmony said later.

'Because it was unPersonlike?'

'No. Because it was an affront to his dignity. We don't want to make enemies.'

'I don't think Polly bears malice,' I said. 'Anyway, he was insulting you. I'm not standing for that.'

Harmony smiled.

'And if he as much as lays a finger on you. . . .' I went on.

'Dear Vector,' she said. 'I can deal with Polly. And you're more Personlike than you think, though not as Personlike as you used to be, I'm glad to say. In spite of which' – she kissed me – 'I like being rallied round by you. I love you. As I intend to show you, one of these days.'

'When?' I inquired gloomily.

We were in fact, for once, by ourselves in a room, although the buzz of voices from the adjoining room was a reminder that we didn't have any reliable privacy. Maggie and Tom, Candy and Tigger were holding the weekly meeting at which they discussed the progress of the Community's various activities. Harmony and I were not included in this discussion, and Polly, who rarely bothered with it, was out in the city.

'Not just now, I'm afraid,' Harmony said, answering my question. 'Still, we don't have to be *too* self-restrained. We must take such opportunities as we have.'

Then we had our arms round each other. The strange delightful feelings I'd first experienced in the Precinct – was it only two or three weeks ago? – came crowding back, accompanied by some disturbing new thoughts. For some time I'd supposed myself to be a full male, but was it possible I was deceiving myself? Was a full male actually a Person like Polly, who could boast of his successes with females? Was I even sure I was capable of physical love-making – and if not, would I cruelly disappoint Harmony when the time came? That would be a dreadful thing to do to her.

'Even Creatures mate,' I said aloud.

'Creatures love,' Harmony said.

'Oh, come now, that's going too far.'

'It's not. I go into Creature homes, you know, for my work. Creatures love their children, and parents, and friends. And they make love to their partners, of course they do.'

'You don't see *that*, I'm sure.'

'I don't need to see it, I *know* it. We say Creatures aren't like us, but I sometimes wish we were more like them.'

I had a sudden picture of us as an observer might have glimpsed us at that moment: no longer the clean, well-dressed, smooth-skinned Persons we'd been in the Colony, but a rough, barefoot pair in coarse clothing, twined together on a bench in a bleak room lit by a single candle. We might indeed have been mistaken at a casual glance for Creatures. At one time the thought would have horrified me. Now I found it surprisingly close to being acceptable.

'How long can we go on like this?' I asked.

'In the Community, you mean?'

'Yes. We aren't getting anywhere, are we? We haven't found Melody and we aren't together, not properly.'

'I ask about Melody wherever I go,' Harmony said. 'I still feel sure she's alive. And I still think the Community people know something about her and eventually we'll hear it.'

'I wish we could leave and live together, just the two of us.'

'Maybe we will, in time. But how would we manage? I don't earn much. The customers are so poor.'

'And I don't earn anything,' I admitted. 'I can clean a house and light fires and feed rabbits and weed a vegetable patch. But that's not much use unless we have a house to clean and rabbits to feed and a patch to weed.'

'I think we'll have to stay for the time being. Perhaps when we've found Melody, though....'

'*If* we find Melody....'

We became silent. I was tired after my day's work and fell into a doze, as I think Harmony did too. The sense of frustration faded. Still clasped in each other's arms, we shared a dream of being permanently together. Then the buzz of voices next door changed tone and the door handle rattled. We shot apart.

Maggie strode towards us, a smile on her usually-unsmiling face. The other members followed her and stood around.

'Well, Hatty and Vic,' she said, 'we've made a decision. We're admitting you to full membership of the Community. We're pleased with the way you've settled down to life here, and we feel you are promising colleagues. We hope your stay with us will be long and happy.'

'In other words,' said Tom, 'you're in. And....'

'Allow me, Tom!' Maggie said. 'We've also decided that this is the time to make another change. We've been dissatisfied for a long time with Polly's attitudes and behaviour. So....'

'So Polly's out!' said Tom.

Maggie glared at him. 'So it's been resolved,' she said, 'that as from tomorrow Polly is no longer a member of the Community. We shall give him time to make other arrangements, of course, but we shall expect him to leave us within the next few days.'

Maggie had pitched her voice rather high while making the announcements, but now she dropped it to a more normal note. 'It'll make a bit more space in the men's sleeping quarters,' she added. 'You've been rather crowded, haven't you, since Vic came?'

Something in her face told me there was one respect in which she was determined the Community wouldn't change. It was still not going to be a love-nest.

Then Polly came in. He was a little unsteady. It looked as if he'd been at the parsnip ale again.

'Well, Polly,' said Maggie, 'you've chosen your moment well. I have something to tell you.' And she told him.

There was a moment's silence.

Then, 'You take the words from my mouth, my dear Maggie,' Polly said. 'I was about to inform you to the same effect. I've decided I have no further use for the Community. I cannot see that its existence is of any benefit to anyone.'

'We set an example,' said Maggie, tight-lipped. 'An example of hard work and self-help. We hope there'll be some who follow it.'

'Ah, well, setting an example is not in my line,' said Polly. 'Not a *good* example, anyway. I shall go on my way rejoicing. I've been offered a room at the Red Lion which I shall accept immediately. I've no wish to see any of you ever again. Except' – his eye fell on Harmony – 'except perhaps one.'

'You keep well away from *her*!' I said.

Chapter Eleven

I was lifting potatoes a few days later when Harmony came out to me.

'Vector!' she said. 'I've been thinking about Polly.'

'Oh?' I said. 'Why think about Polly? *I* don't.'

'Because of this conspiracy of silence about Melody. Now he's not in the Community, we might get him to talk.'

'Well, yes, I suppose we might,' I said without much enthusiasm.

'He's usually at the tavern by late afternoon. Let's go round and see him tomorrow.'

'I have my work to do.'

'You can take a bit of time out.'

That was true. The house and garden were well tended and I was in good odour. Nobody would complain if I was absent for a while.

'Come with me on my round,' Harmony went on. She was well established by now, and Maggie had ceased to accompany her. Her practice was to deliver finished manuscripts each afternoon and collect new orders, which she would work on in the evening and the following morning.

Next day I hurried through my work. Soon after lunch the cups, bowls and spoons were all washed and the whole place was immaculate. I joined Harmony and we went out through the big wooden gate. It was the first time I'd been outside the Community's grounds since my arrival there, and I felt slightly nervous. But such Creatures as we saw in the streets seemed harmless enough, and some of them exchanged greetings with Harmony.

We went to several dwellings, where documents she had written out were accepted with gratitude and some awe. Payment was made with apologies for its not being enough. Some of Harmony's customers who had no money paid her with scraps of food.

When all the work had been delivered and new orders picked up, Harmony said, 'Well, I should think by now Polly will be at the Red Lion.'

'What *is* a lion, by the way?'

'An imaginary animal, I think. There's a picture of one on a sign outside the tavern.'

'Do you know the way?'

'I think so. Actually, you can hear that tavern from two or three streets away.'

We did indeed hear the tavern before we reached it. Rough male Creature voices were raised in joke and argument. There were no females present, and I had some doubt whether it was wise for Harmony to be there. But it was still daylight, and I had no sense of anything sinister about the place, though I didn't like the smells of fermented drink and urine, or the garbage which lay in piles in the street in front.

As we approached, there were two or three of the peculiar loud whistles with which the male Creatures were apt to indicate sexual interest, and when Harmony blushed there were two or three more. Inside the wide open door was a counter across which drink was passed in exchange for the small coins with which I'd now become familiar, or for some small possession.

Polly was there. His tall, bulky figure loomed above the rest, and he was talking loudly to those around him in fluent colloquial Creature. He came to us at once and flung an arm around each of us.

'My dear young friends!' he greeted us. 'Has life in the Community become too much for you already? Come and have a change from it. Allow me to buy you a drink. I recommend, if that isn't too encouraging a word, the parsnip ale, which is fairly potent and slightly less vile than most of the stuff they sell here.'

He rapped on the counter, and a Creature girl brought cups of an obnoxious brew of which I could drink no more than a mouthful. Polly bought drink also for several of the Creatures around him.

'And now,' he said expansively, 'is there anything I can do for you, other than make you drunk?'

'You can tell us what you know about Melody,' Harmony said abruptly.

'Melody! Well, well. What makes you think I know anything about Melody? Or, indeed, who Melody is? Or was?'

'You do, don't you?' said Harmony. 'I'm sure everyone in the Community knows about Melody, but they won't tell us.'

'Now let me see,' said Polly. He paused, as if searching the recesses of his memory. Then he beamed, with an air of sudden discovery, and said, 'Actually I do seem to remember something about some such Person. But why do *you* want to know?'

'You must know that,' Harmony said. 'I'm her sister. I want to find her.'

'Yes, of course.' Polly emptied his glass of parsnip ale and pushed it across the counter for a refill. 'Very natural.' He paused. We both looked at him expectantly.

'Well, she's still alive,' he said at length.

Harmony gave a sigh of relief. 'And where is she?'

'Don't go too fast, my dear. I seem to recall that I gave a promise to the Community members not to talk about her.'

'I shouldn't have thought that would stop you,' I said rudely.

Polly was not offended. 'Perhaps not,' he said. 'It's merely slowing me down a little. Well, for a start, I can tell you she was once in the Community herself.'

'I thought so, somehow,' Harmony said. 'Why did she leave?'

'She did something the other members disapproved of. Strongly disapproved of. I wasn't there at the time, but I heard about it. It was something they thought put the Community in peril. They're a timid lot, you know.' He paused again, eyeing Harmony appreciatively. 'How charming you are, my dear. Truly charming.'

'What did she do and where is she?' demanded Harmony, brushing the compliment aside.

'Aha,' said Polly. 'You really do want to know, don't you, my dear?'

'Of course I do,' Harmony said.

'Then I dare say it can be arranged.'

We both stared.

'What do you mean?' Harmony asked.

'I mean,' said Polly amiably, 'that if you will come to my room at a suitable time I'll tell you all I know.'

'When? Now?'

'Why not?' said Polly.

'I'll come too,' I said.

'Oh, no, my dear Vector, no. I'm afraid you are not invited.'

Harmony and I both gasped as the implications of what he'd said began to sink in.

'Please,' said Harmony. 'I appeal to you. Tell me about my sister.'

'That's just what I propose to do. I've given you an invitation, a sincere invitation. I hope you'll accept it in a suitable spirit and – dare I say it? – a suitable mood.'

I remembered a phrase I'd learned from Node, back in the Precinct.

'You bastard!' I said. 'You utter bastard!'

Polly laughed delightedly.

'Your command of Creature is better than I thought, Vector,' he said. And then, 'Think it over, Harmony my dear. There's no hurry. At least, for me there's no hurry. You'll be just as nice next week as now.'

'I'm not doing it!' Harmony declared.

'Don't be hasty!' Polly advised her. 'It might take you a long time to find Melody by any other means.'

'You are detestable!' Harmony said, turned her back on him, and walked out. I went after her. Polly's laughter followed us half-way down the street.

'You won't go, will you?' I said.

'I will not.' A moment's hesitation. Then, 'But Vector, do you think perhaps I should?'

'No, I don't. You know what his intentions are.'

'He can't actually force me.'

'He won't tell you anything unless he gets what he wants.' And another thought struck me. 'He might not tell you anything even then. He may not even *know* anything when it comes to the point.'

We walked on, dismayed.

'As he says, it could take a long time,' Harmony said. 'This is a big city.'

'But if she *is* alive there have to be people who know her,' I said, trying to be cheerful, 'and sooner or later we'll run across one of them. It could be any moment.'

At that point I realized that somebody was following us and catching up rapidly. I was alarmed. I had no defensive weapon, and the light was beginning to fade.

'It's all right,' a male voice said. 'It's only me.'

It was a Creature of my own age or a little more: fairly tall as Creatures went, with curly hair and no apparent deformity. I recognized him at once.

'You're Nick,' I said. 'You come to the Community to collect our surplus vegetables.'

'That's right.' He nodded to Harmony. Then, 'I heard what that feller Polly said. Couldn't help it, he was talking so loud. He should go easy on the parsnip ale.'

We waited. Nick paused a moment before going on, 'I might be able to help you.'

'You mean, you know where Melody is?'

'I mean, I'd like you to meet a friend of mine. A friend called Lil.'

'We'd be glad to,' I said. 'But why ... ?'

'She's a Person, you see. A Person that took a Creature name, like they do in the Community.'

Harmony started forward. 'What was her Person name, Nick?'

'I dunno. I only know her as Lil.' Nick hesitated, then, 'She looks rather like you. In fact she looks *very* like you.'

'She always did,' said Harmony slowly. And then she was suddenly excited and smiling.

'But this is wonderful!' she declared. 'I just can't believe it. And yet ... Vector, it *must* be her, mustn't it? It has to be. There couldn't be another Person outside who happened to resemble me. Oh, I can't wait to see her!'

She threw her arms round me, and then embraced Nick in turn. I didn't mind; at least, not much.

'What more do you know about her?' Harmony demanded.

'All I know is, she came out of the Precinct three, maybe four years ago. Came of her own accord, I think. They didn't throw her out. She joined the Community.'

'I knew it!' Harmony declared triumphantly. 'Polly said Melody was in the Community. It's as good as proved. Melody is Lil!' And then once more she looked puzzled. 'But why did they deny all knowledge of her?'

'They would!' said Nick. 'They didn't want you having anything to do with her, I reckon. Didn't want to revive the connection. They wanted to forget all about her; keep it dark that she'd ever belonged.'

'Why, Nick, why?'

'I guess they thought she was dangerous. They don't like trouble, you know. She had some wild ideas. And then she got married. . . .'

'How could she?' I asked. 'Who is there out here for a Person to marry?'

'She married a Creature.'

'She *what*?'

'Married a Creature. Len. He's a friend of mine, too.'

I was dumbfounded. 'But that's impossible!' I said faintly.

'Can't be impossible. It happened.'

'It's a biological absurdity.'

'Polly doesn't find it a biological absurdity to go with Creature girls,' Nick remarked.

'That's different,' I said. 'But still disgusting, if you ask me.'

'I don't ask you,' Nick said; and there was something in his tone of voice that made me feel suddenly ashamed of myself. I said no more.

Nick went on, speaking to Harmony, 'They wouldn't have liked it anyway that she married a Creature because in spite of taking Creature names and all that, they feel deep down the same as your friend here. You speak politely to Creatures but you don't actually marry them.'

'Nick, I'm sorry I said that.'

'So you should be,' Harmony told me.

'And they particularly didn't like it that it was Len she married,' said Nick. 'Len's been in trouble with the Guards, see. Making a stand for Creatures' rights. They think he's a revolutionary.'

Chapter Twelve

'Nick, I must go to her,' Harmony said. 'At once, if possible.'

'Sure. I'll take you. Unless you'd rather wait till day-time. They live in the Stumps. It's quite a long walk.'

'I'd rather go now.'

'All right. But ... I haven't told you quite everything yet. Get ready for a shock. Lil's poorly. She's very poorly ... I think she's dying.'

I thought Harmony was going to fall. This reversal of the good news she'd heard only a few minutes ago was too cruel. I put an arm round her. She recovered sufficiently to ask, 'Why? What with?'

'She has consumption.'

'I don't know what that is. It sounds awful.'

'It's a wasting disease.'

'And isn't there any medical help for her?'

'You kidding?' said Nick. From being sympathetic, his voice took on a bitter note. 'What medical treatment is there in this city? There's the Wise Women, and they do their best, but that's all. You have your own doctor, I know, but he's never seen out here.'

Harmony was silent, still in a state of shock. I said defensively, 'What could one doctor do in a city this size?' And then, with spirit, 'Anyway, is it always up to us? Can't your people do anything for themselves?'

'Oh, come off it,' Nick said. 'You must know by now how things are. Filth, bad water, all kinds of diseases. It's a miracle if anyone's healthy here. And where's the medical training? Where's the drugs? Where's the equipment? We haven't had them since the good days went. Don't talk to me like that!'

'I'm sorry, Nick,' I said for the second time.

'That's all right.' Nick's tone was more friendly now. 'Actually you got a point. If nobody helps you, you got to help yourself, right? And I don't just mean doctoring.'

'So when do Creatures start helping themselves?'

'Well now, if it wasn't for Lil being sick, you'd be coming to the right place to find out. But this has hit Len hard. With his life as it is, he can't do much just now. Still, the time may be on its way. . . .'

'King Creature, come, and all that?' I asked.

'Could be.'

'There isn't really a King Creature, is there?'

'Don't be so sure. There might be more in that than you think.'

'You don't really believe it, do you, Nick?'

'Well, there's rumours. Something may have happened that'll set things moving.'

'Please,' said Harmony, 'may we go and find my sister?'

'That's what we're doing,' said Nick. 'This way, down into town.'

'Tell me some more about the rumours,' I said. But I could sense that Nick was drawing back.

'You been in the Precinct till recently,' he said. 'For all I know, you might be in there again tomorrow. If I did know anything, do you think I'd tell you about it, just like that? Think again, brother. Maybe I told you too much already.'

'You can trust us, Nick,' said Harmony.

'I better, hadn't I?' But Nick said nothing more; and soon afterwards he signalled to us to be quiet.

We were picking our way through narrow, winding streets. Hardly anyone was out of doors now. Lights flickered from within the barred window-spaces of dwellings. A nearly-full moon slid from cloud to cloud, and there were occasional drops of rain in the wind.

'Would we be safer in the main streets?' I asked.

'Keep your voice down. No, we wouldn't. Only gangs go in the main streets. If there was twenty of us and we were looking for trouble, we would. But there isn't twenty of us and we're not looking for trouble.'

And when we had to cross a main street, Nick approached the

junction cautiously and peered in all directions before signing to us to move swiftly ahead.

By now the streets were becoming broader anyway, though still deserted. I was sure we were approaching the city centre. Nick confirmed it.

'This is City Square,' he whispered. 'And there's the Stumps, over there.'

The square was a large open space. The moon, making one of its appearances, showed us a representation of a four-legged animal with the torso and limbs of a human-looking figure mounted on it.

'A horse and rider, isn't it?' I asked. 'What's it for?'

'It's just a statue. Some feller that was supposed to have saved his country in the good days.' Nick laughed soundlessly. 'He lost his head years ago. Come on, we'll sneak round the edge of the square. The middle of it's a bit too exposed for my liking.'

Soon we were in reach of the cluster of buildings called the Stumps. Then Nick signalled to us to keep back. The way was blocked by a gang. Half-crouching, we peered at it from round a corner.

The gang consisted mostly of young males, though there also appeared to be two or three skinny females; I couldn't easily distinguish them. They were shouting and jeering at each other, and passing round two or three of the rolled cylinders I'd seen on my first morning outside. The lit ends of the cylinders glowed, brightening and fading in the dark. The gang didn't appear to be doing anything except passing time.

Nick sank to his haunches on the sidewalk. 'We'll just have to wait,' he said softly.

'Would they really attack us, if we walked openly to where we're going?' Harmony asked.

'Ssssh. Yes, most likely they would.'

We were silent. Time passed. No one set foot in the square except a pair of uniformed Guards walking in step, their boots echoing on the paving. They ignored the gang, and the gang ignored them. Eventually, for no obvious reason, the gang began to move in a slow, disorganized fashion towards us.

Nick signalled again, and we retreated silently round the nearest corner. The members of the gang straggled past. Seen from closer quarters they looked pathetic: thin and ill-clad, and many of them poor physical specimens. But I didn't doubt that they could be nasty. A few of them carried sticks, and one or two had lengths of rusty chain wrapped round their fists. We waited until they were well out of the way, then walked towards the nearest of the Stumps.

It was a block of dwellings, looking like a poor imitation of our own Towers, though I remembered that according to Helix the Stumps were actually older than anything of ours on this planet. From the roof of the bare lobby hung a flickering lantern.

'There's a surprise for you,' Nick said. 'They don't often stay alight as long as this. Get things thrown at them. We're lucky for once. You have to watch out, going into this place in the dark.'

We climbed up countless concrete steps, going round and round a dark well. Rubbish littered the steps, and you had to watch what you trod in. There was a pervasive stink. Feeble light from the lantern threw wavering shadows on the walls.

After half a dozen flights, Nick halted. 'Len!' he bawled, in an ear-splitting voice. 'Len! Len!'

Somewhere above, a door opened and a little light leaked out. 'Who is it?'

'It's me. Nick. I brought someone to see you.'

'Come on up. Not too much noise when you get inside. She's poorly.'

As soon as we were in the apartment, Len shot a heavy bolt behind us. The room we were in was very small, and lit by the usual single candle. I saw in its light that Len was a fully grown Creature of average height – that is, a little shorter than Harmony or myself – and of slight though wiry build. His hair was dark and thick, his voice a little harsh. He looked desperate.

'Things are bad, Nick, that's the truth,' he said. 'Come in and see her.'

There was a second room opening out of the first. In it a female lay on some kind of couch, covered with a grey blanket. She was asleep, but muttering to herself. Her face was gaunt, a whitish-grey except for bright patches of red on her cheeks, and there were tiny beads of sweat on her forehead.

Harmony hesitated. For a few moments I felt she wasn't sure she recognized the woman's face. It was hard to see a resemblance now.

Then she was down on her knees beside the couch, weeping.

Everyone was silent, not wanting to wake the sleeping woman. Len studied me in some bafflement. I was shaken, as much by him as by the sight of illness, which itself was new to me. Though I'd received many shocks in the past few weeks, it was still barely credible to me that a Person could be paired with a Creature. And, said a small, cold, unpleasant voice somewhere inside me, look what it has brought her to.

After some time the woman stirred and opened her eyes. The irises were colourless. Harmony's face was close to hers. She stared and half sat up.

'Who is it?' she asked.

'Harmony.'

'Who?'

'Harmony.'

'You're a Person, aren't you?'

'I'm your sister. I'm Harmony. Oh, Melody, my dear, I'm your sister. You understand? Your sister.'

Even now it took a little time for the woman to grasp the truth. At length I saw recognition dawn in her face. She struggled to a sitting position. Harmony rose from her knees, sat on the couch, and stretched out her arms. Melody was smiling, painfully.

'I never thought I'd see you again,' she said. But in a moment she was racked with a fit of coughing, and held a piece of crumpled cloth to her mouth.

The agony in Len's face was all too plain. And the feeling that I'd first had when I watched the Creature being manhandled by Guards came over me again, but much more strongly: an overwhelming sense of shared humanity.

'C'mon, fellers,' Nick whispered. 'We better leave them to it.' And quietly the three of us withdrew.

It seemed hours before Harmony joined us. In the interval we didn't talk much. I had the impression that Len and Nick might have had much more to say to each other if I hadn't been there, but that they didn't entirely trust me. I couldn't blame them. I knew Len had been in trouble with the Guards, and probably Nick too was a campaigner for Creature rights. No doubt that was a risky business.

Len was quite friendly, though. He made a hot drink, which I swallowed without grimacing, and later he rolled a cylinder with the dried, herbal-looking stuff inside. We drew on it in turn. I sensed that these things were scarce and dear, and I didn't enjoy it anyway, but it seemed important to share in the rite.

Low voices came through to us from the adjoining room, and occasionally a burst of coughing, at which Len winced. Then there was silence for some time, and eventually the door opened and Harmony came out. Her eyes were dry now.

'She's asleep again,' she said. 'I'm staying here for the time being if you don't mind, Len. And you, Vic, had better go straight to the Precinct, to tell the doctor.'

'He's on vacation,' I said. 'At the Summer Valley.'

'Never mind. There'll be somebody at the health centre. They can send a land-craft and take Melody in. She'll be comfortable and cared for, and they can bring Rhombus back from the Summer Valley in the morning.'

'I've tried the Precinct already,' said Len. 'She didn't want me to, but when she got really bad I did. It wasn't any good, though. The Guards wouldn't let me in or take a message or anything.'

'Surely they'll do something for Vector,' Harmony said.

'Because he's a Person,' said Nick.

'I don't look much like a Person at the moment,' I said. 'And they didn't treat the Community members like Persons, remember.'

'It'll be different at the Precinct itself,' said Harmony. 'Ask for the Guard Commander. If we're lucky it'll be Node. But whoever's on duty, explain what's needed, and if there are any difficulties ask him to send for a senior Person. They've *got* to do something about this. Off you go, Vic. Please.'

I wasn't as confident as Harmony. But I couldn't have refused to go.

'All right,' I said. 'And the sooner the better.'

'I'll take you to the gate,' Nick offered.

Len rose to let us out. As he did so, there was a knock at the door. 'Who is it?' he called.

'It's me. Rose.'

Len opened up. A middle-aged woman stood in the doorway

with a small child whom she propelled in front of her into the room.

'Here's your treasure,' the woman said. 'She's been as good as gold all day. Good-night, my precious. Good-night, all.' Stepping back, she closed the door again.

The child was a little girl.

Wide, dark Creature eyes.

A cloud of pale, fine, spun-gold hair.

She ran to Len, who put his arms round her and lifted her to his knee.

'This is Sarah,' he said. 'Serenade to you.'

'Come on, Vic,' said Nick. 'Don't stare like you seen a ghost. Let's be getting you to that gate.'

Chapter Thirteen

Outside, it had started to rain.

'Best weather for moving around in at night,' said Nick. 'Gets the lads off the streets.' And our journey across the city was uneventful. It wasn't long before we were walking briskly up the last steep street that led to the Precinct.

'I'll leave you here,' Nick said when the gate came into view. 'It won't help you to have a Creature with you. Might not be too healthy for *me*, neither. Len and me, we aren't popular with the Guards. See you again, Vic, I hope.'

The main airlock of course was closed at this hour. There was a small one beside it, at the entrance to which stood a uniformed Guard, thickset and pugnacious-looking.

'Off you go!' he said.

'I want to come in, Guard.'

'Nothing doing. You know you don't get in at this time of night.'

'It's important. There's a Person, very ill, outside.'

'Don't try to tell me that. There's no Persons gone outside today.'

'It's true, Guard. She's been outside a long time. Listen, I'm a Person myself. Can't you tell from my voice?'

'I don't care who you are. Persons that's gone permanently outside aren't Persons no more, them's our instructions. Clear off quick, before I give you something to remember me by.'

'Who's the Guard Commander on duty?'

'It's Root. But you don't get to see him.'

'Listen, I tell you, this is a case of sickness. It's serious.'

'GET OUT!'

I was furious by now.

'It's an outrage!' I began. 'You'll hear more....'

The Guard went to the small gate and called to a couple of his fellow Guards inside. In a moment my position was roughly that of the Creature I'd seen being ill-treated here, a lifetime ago as it now seemed. The three of them took it in turns to hit me. Then I was pushed along with kicks and blows, and finally the Guard I had first spoken to sent me off in the direction of the city by landing his heavy boot in my backside.

Dizzy, sore, and above all bewildered, I staggered away down the hill until I was out of sight of the gate. Then I stopped and thought. Node had to be in charge of one of the three shifts at the guardroom. He would recognize me and let me in. I was not going to be defeated. I would keep going back until I made it.

It was still raining, and there was no obvious shelter around, but I found a doorway and curled myself up in it. It didn't give much protection, but I was wet through anyway. Soaked, bruised and aching, and with my mind reeling from the day's experiences, I didn't expect to get much sleep. Yet I fell into a series of dozes that took me through the night, until I was awakened in the grey, damp dawn by the sound of a squad of Guards marching past me towards the city.

The rain had dwindled to a few drops borne on a light wind. Creatures in ones and twos were moving up the hill towards the Precinct. I followed them. When I got there the main airlock was still closed. The Guard at the smaller gate had changed, I was glad to see; the new one was thin, tall for a Creature, and very young-looking. And he was surrounded by half a dozen Creatures whose voices were raised in indignation.

'No work!' one of them shouted angrily. 'What do you mean, no work? We get here at this time and you tell us there's no work!'

'That's my instructions,' the young Guard said defensively. 'Come back tomorrow. There might be something for you then.'

'But listen, we *must* be first. They can't have given out the work already!'

'I didn't say they had. I just said there's no work today.'

'No work!' The words were bandied disgustedly around the little group of people, and thrown at new arrivals.

'Who says?' demanded somebody truculently. 'We don't take it from *him*, do we?'

The noise level increased as the Guard was surrounded by more and more Creatures. Before long he spoke into a miniature caller. Then he said to the crowd, 'The Guard Commander's on his way. He'll tell you.'

I hung back on the fringe. A few minutes passed, during which the crowd continued to grow and became more angry and impatient.

Then the Guard Commander appeared through the small gate. To my vast relief it was Node. He was confident, fully in charge, looking as if the Precinct belonged to him personally. When he held up a hand for silence, the hubbub diminished at once, and somebody at the back who continued to protest was hushed by those around him.

'The Guard has told you,' Node proclaimed in a firm voice, 'that there is no work today. You all understand plain language. I'm telling you again, and you can take it from me. There is NO WORK.'

'Why?' somebody demanded.

'That's not your business,' said Node briskly. 'You've been told you can come back tomorrow. There may be work as usual then. I'm not promising. Now go away. Tell everyone you meet on the way down.'

But the throng remained around him, unwilling to disperse.

'I give you two minutes,' said Node. 'Then we clear the area. You know what that means.'

Still muttering, the crowd broke up and began to drift away down the hill. Two or three individuals hung behind at a safe distance, as if unwilling to believe that there wouldn't be a small amount of work for those who waited long enough.

As Node turned to go into the Precinct, I stepped forward. The young Guard motioned me back.

'You heard!' he said.

'Node!' I called. 'Node!'

The Guard Commander turned, looked in my direction, but didn't respond.

'Node!' I cried again, more loudly.

'Get rid of him!' Node told the young Guard.

I ran forward.

'Node!' I yelled. 'You know me! It's Vector! I've got to speak to you, Node. A life and death matter.'

Node looked me up and down coldly, without any sign of recognition.

'I don't know who or what you are,' he said. 'I've never seen you before and I don't want to see you again. And whoever you are, GET AWAY FROM THIS GATE!'

'You *do* know me!' I burst out. 'Node, it's important! It's urgent! It's about Harmony, and Melody!'

'Creatures have been shot,' said Node, 'for less impudence than that. Guard, you may take whatever measures are needed to clear him out of the way. As for *you*' – turning to me – 'I give you a final warning. Go while the going's good!'

He turned on his heel and went into the Precinct. I stood for a while, dismayed and defeated, feeling that there must be some extraordinary mistake, but unable to make any sense out of events.

'You heard him,' said the young Guard. 'Don't make me do what I don't want to do.' His tone was almost one of appeal. I turned and moved dispiritedly away down the hill.

It was light by now, and there were people out in the streets. Women lined up at the taps; smoke rose from some of the chimneys. Children, scantily clad for this cold, damp, autumn weather, squatted or crawled or ran about. Here and there, little groups of adults stood talking; from the words I picked up it was clear that the lack of work at the Precinct was already a major topic. No one knew what to make of it.

The distance to the city centre didn't seem great. As I crossed the square, passing by the figure of the man on horseback, I thought I recognized the back view of a tall Creature wearing bright stitched-together rags of many colours. I overtook her and looked into the gaunt, hollow-eyed face.

'Hello!' I said. 'You're Em Briggs. The Wise Woman!'

'That's right,' the Wise Woman said in her strange, resonant voice. 'You're the young Person I met at Vi's, three or four weeks ago.'

'I'm glad I've seen you,' I said. 'Will you come to somebody who's very ill? It's not far. This first block ahead of us.'

'You mean Lil? I'm going to see her right now.'

'You never told me you attended another Person.'

'I don't tell everyone my business. Specially when they've just come from the Precinct, as you had then. The Precinct to us means Guards, and Guards mean trouble.'

'I've nothing to do with any Guards,' I said, thinking bitterly of Node, whom I'd supposed to be my friend.

'And I don't look on Lil as a Person,' the Wise Woman added. 'She's one of us now. Poor soul.'

We went into the first of the Stumps and made our way up the evil-smelling staircase. Len opened the apartment door to us.

'She's a bit better this morning,' he said. In the inner room, Melody was propped up in a sitting position and was talking with some degree of animation to Harmony, who once again sat beside her on the couch.

Harmony sprang up. 'Well?' she said. 'When are they coming?'

But she could see at once from my face that I'd failed. Her own face clouded. 'What happened?' she asked.

'They wouldn't let me in.'

'Come out here,' Harmony said.

We left the Wise Woman with Len and Melody while we talked in the outer room. I told Harmony what had happened.

'But that's dreadful!' she said.

'According to the Guard on duty last night,' I told her, 'a Person who goes outside stops being a Person. I suppose that ruling must come from higher up. Perhaps if you leave the Colony you cease to exist, officially, and can't be recognized.'

'It's possible,' Harmony said. 'After all, nobody ever talked about Melody.'

'Or about the people who set up the Community. It's as if they hadn't existed. Maybe I don't exist now.'

'But I should have thought Helix or Node would have warned us of that,' said Harmony. 'Anyway, where does it leave us? What do we do now?'

'Well. . . .' I said. There was a long, significant silence.

'Yes, I know,' said Harmony. 'I shall have to go myself.'

'Well, it's my guess that they'll let *you* in. You're valuable.'

'Yes,' said Harmony. 'And you know what else?'

I did. 'I know all too well,' I said. 'Once you're back in there, they'll never let you out again. And they'll never let *me* in. It will be the end for us.'

She nodded. Then she put her arms round my neck.

We stayed clasped together for some minutes. It was the second such crisis we had faced, and worse than the first one.

'What will happen to Melody if we don't get medical care for her?' I asked.

'She'll die.'

Death. That was a subject Persons rarely talked about. If we did have to mention it, we preferred to call it cessation. And it had never come close to me. No one had ceased in the Colony while I was there. Persons went Home to Annulus before they reached ceasing age. They must cease eventually, one supposed, but they would do so in peace and quiet, and in privacy. In the Colony, serious accident and illness were almost unknown. Everyone was far too careful. Rhombus, the doctor, had little more to do than anyone else in the Colony; his health centre, adjoining the Bowling Green, treated mainly Guards and their families.

In such a way of life, one didn't quite believe that cessation would ever happen to oneself; one felt immortal. It was at that moment in Len's apartment that it first came home to me that I would die myself; that some day Harmony would die.

This enormous thought had just taken possession of my mind when the Wise Woman emerged.

'Well?' said Harmony.

'Not too good. She's less feverish, but that's usual in the mornings with this disease. The fever gets worse as the day goes on.'

'And what are her chances?' I asked, hoping against hope.

The Wise Woman looked away. Len, who had come out of the inner room with her, looked away in another direction so that their eyes didn't meet. There was silence. I didn't press for an answer.

'Is there anything that would cure her?' I asked instead.

'At this stage? I don't know, my dear. I'm only the Wise Woman, and not as wise as some of them think. In the good days they used to cure consumption, I'm told, but now we haven't the art. With matters the way they are, there's only one thing that would give her a chance. She needs fresh country air and rest and plenty of wholesome food.'

'She might as well need the moon,' said Len bitterly.

'Supposing we got her back into the Precinct?' Harmony said.

'Oh, well, that's another matter. They have drugs and all sorts of treatments there, I believe. I dare say they could cure her. If you could get her in there, you should.'

'You didn't have any luck, did you, Vic?' Len asked.

'No.'

'*I* might,' said Harmony. 'But oh, if I go back in. . . .' Her face was stricken. 'If I go back in, they'll keep me there.'

If I'd stopped to think about it, I might have made a more selfish decision than I did. But my mind was still staggering under the weight of the thought of death. I couldn't just let it happen to the woman – Harmony's sister – who was sick right here in this apartment now, if there was any possibility of transforming her into the proper clean healthy beautiful being that a Person ought to be. And I couldn't expect Harmony just to let it happen, either.

'You must do what you can for your sister,' I said.

'Yes,' said Harmony. 'Yes.' A long silence. 'I shall try to get away again, Vector, you know I will. If I don't make it, it won't be for lack of trying. Come with me to the gate.'

With Harmony I walked yet again across the city. I was getting to know the way by heart. At the first sight of the gate we embraced briefly and I dropped back; both of us felt, I think, that if we didn't part swiftly we would never be able to tear ourselves apart at all.

The young, round-faced Guard was still on duty, which suggested that Node would still be on duty, too. Node had been close to Harmony for years and to all appearances had loved, almost worshipped her. He *could* not reject her. This gave me a kind of comfort but a great deal more agony.

The main airlock was open now, and I watched Harmony's tall, slim figure walking away from me towards it, and wondered if this was the last time I would see her. The Guard stepped forward to intercept her. They stood talking for a minute or two; then both of them moved inside and out of my sight.

I lingered, half hoping and half fearing that she would reappear. If she was admitted to the Precinct, it was likely that help would be sent for Melody but that Harmony herself would be lost to me. If she reappeared it would indicate failure: Harmony and I would still be together, but Melody would die, leaving her man, her child, her sister ... I didn't know which possibility was the more dreadful.

And then Harmony was outside the gate again, running towards me. 'Vector!' she cried. 'What's happening? Node pretended not to know *me*, either. He'd never seen me before, he didn't know or care who I was, and if I didn't leave of my own accord he'd tell the Guards to use their own way of getting rid of me! Has he gone mad?'

'No, he's not gone mad,' I said. 'I think my guess must be right. They're under instructions not to let us in, or even to recognize us.'

'But why, why, why?' Harmony asked. 'And what can we do about Melody now?'

I was silent because I couldn't think of anything. Slowly we walked down into the city centre. The problem of a month earlier had been reversed. Then we had been in the Precinct trying to find a way out. Now we were outside trying to find a way in; and this time we didn't have the help of Node.

'I suppose we'd better go back to the Community,' Harmony said.

'*They* won't do anything for us.'

'I know they won't. But we're still members. And they haven't seen us since yesterday afternoon. They'll be wondering what's happened to us.'

'They've got some explaining to do,' I said grimly. 'Preventing you from finding out about your own sister! I shall tell them what I think of that!'

Harmony sighed. 'It won't do any good,' she said. 'And at the moment we've nowhere else to live. Len and Melody don't have room for us.'

'We're not staying in the Community. We'll find a place of our own somehow. Let's just tell them we're going, and pick up our belongings. That won't take long!'

We went on our way, heading now for the East Quarter. The

gate to the courtyard stood open. No one was to be seen. And some instinct of caution stopped us half-way across the yard. I put a finger to my lips.

There were voices from inside the house. Guard voices. Person voices, protesting. The sound of a blow. A cry of pain. And, then, emerging, the squad of Guards I'd seen marching down the hill at dawn. With them, bound at the wrists and being roughly pushed along, were the four remaining members of the Community: Maggie, Candy, Tom and Tigger.

We had just time to dart round the corner of the outhouse. We didn't venture to peep out until they had gone past and were out of earshot. There was nothing we could do. A rescue bid was out of the question.

'It's just one thing after another, isn't it!' Harmony exclaimed.

'If we'd been there, I expect *we'd* have been arrested!' I said. 'I wonder what it's all about.'

'I don't know, but I feel so *helpless*.'

'It's not like you to be helpless,' I said. And the next moment Harmony exclaimed,

'The Summer Valley! Rhombus is spending the autumn there, you said. We must go there and appeal to him directly. And we can see Fulcrum, the sub-Regent, and tell him what's going on because I'm sure the Persons in the Colony don't know about the awful things the Guards keep doing!'

'It's a long way to the Summer Valley,' I said. 'I don't know how we'll get there.'

But even as I said it I was thinking that it would be hard for anyone to keep us out of the Summer Valley. It had a much longer perimeter than the Precinct; and because it was in high hill country, away from the city's seething mass of potential thieves and violent gangs, it was far less closely guarded. I'd been there often on vacation. I was sure I could get in.

I knew Rhombus well, too, and was on good terms with him. I couldn't believe he would refuse to attend a sick Person. I even knew where he was likely to be found. If he wasn't in his holiday apartment, he would be out on the lake in his water-craft.

And finally, although the Guards at the Precinct hadn't shown any interest in us, I couldn't help feeling that with the Community members arrested we might well be in danger ourselves. It would do no harm to get out of the city for a while.

Harmony was looking expectantly at me.

'A great idea!' I said. 'We'll get there, even if we have to walk. And yes, we must go and see Fulcrum. It's high time somebody was told the Guards are getting out of hand. They'll have to be stopped throwing their weight about!'

Chapter Fourteen

'Who's going to stop the Guards throwing their weight about?' inquired a voice at the Community House gate, just behind us. It was Nick. Yes, of course. He'd come to pick up the vegetables which I ought to have had ready for him.

We told him what had happened and what we were hoping to do. He whistled in dismay at the news of the arrests. Then he said, 'You're right. Got to do something about that. To say nothing of poor Lil. But you won't find it easy, getting to the Summer Valley. It's fifty or sixty kilometres the other side of the farm belt, and there's no proper roads up there.'

'Got any suggestions, Nick?'

Nick was thoughtful. After a minute he said, 'Well, beyond the farm belt you're on your own. But I can think of a way of getting as far as that. Arthur.'

'Who's Arthur?'

'Arthur buys the stuff off me that I buy off you. He has a craft, see, a land-craft. It's his living. Now Arthur goes up to one of the farms pretty regular. His cousin's the farmer's wife. They sell him a bit of what ought by rights to go to the Precinct. It's good business, but kind of unofficial. Arthur might be going up there today, or if he isn't I might persuade him. He'd give you a ride, especially if you was to pay him for it. He's not a bad fellow, though I wouldn't trust him too far. And after that his cousins might put you on your way.'

'I thought farmers tended to be friendly with the Guards,' I said doubtfully.

'That's true. But this pair are breaking the rules. They won't want to attract notice, any more than the poor old Community did. Anyway, you got a better idea?'

'No,' I admitted.

'Right. Well, I know where to find Arthur. You go back to Len's apartment, and all being well he'll pick you up there later today.'

Arthur arrived in the middle of the afternoon. I was glad to see him. Len was out looking for work, the child was in the care of the woman they called Rose, and Melody was not so well as she had been earlier in the day. After talking for a while to Harmony she had fallen asleep. There was nothing Harmony and I could do except talk in low voices about the problems ahead and the possible fate of the Community members – a fate which we might ourselves be in danger of sharing.

Arthur was a small, plump, cheerful-looking man. He wore a Guard uniform without any insignia, and was anxious to impress on us that he wasn't a Guard but was only a licensed Creature, allowed in the Precinct to make deliveries. In exchange for Harmony's remaining money he was willing enough to take us to his cousins' farm.

'I been in the Precinct today, as a matter of fact,' he remarked. 'There was some kind of fuss going on. Couldn't get the craft unloaded at first; there wasn't no casual labour. Me and a pair of kitchen Creatures did the unloading in the end. I wouldn't be surprised if a crate or two got lost in the process.' He winked.

'There was something odd when I was there,' I said. 'Everyone was turned away from the gate without work.'

'Some poor Creatures in trouble, most like,' said Arthur. 'It's thieving usually that leads to it. They know the risk, but they do it just the same. I think I heard shots, quite a lot of shots. Maybe a whole gang got caught.'

My heart bumped. I thought once more of the Community members.

'Ah, well, folk got to live, haven't they?' Arthur went on. 'If there's no other way, they thieve. Stands to reason. Come on now, get in the front, there's plenty of room.'

There was indeed room for all three of us side by side in the front of the craft. Arthur set it in motion and headed out of town. Unladen, the craft went at a fairly rapid pace. Arthur kept it bouncing along regardless of ruts and pot-holes, and in spite of his sympathy with thieves he showed little regard for Creature life and limb. He hooted loudly as we approached walkers, and laughed heartily as they leaped out of the way. Sometimes an infirm or elderly Creature would cause him to brake or swerve, and then he would shout out words which were not in our vocabulary of Creature but which we assumed to express strong disapproval.

The road surface got steadily worse, though I guessed that at some time far in the past it had been good. We were moving out of the city now, through a waste land spattered with rough huts, some of them occupied by Creatures and some apparently by hens or rabbits. In several patches of ground we could see vegetables growing. Two or three times we saw primitive craft drawn by long-eared, grey beasts; Arthur referred to these as donkey-carts and shouted words of greeting or disapproval at their drivers according to the speed at which they got out of his way.

'Peasants!' he remarked contemptuously.

'What do they do with the food they grow?'

'Feed themselves, mostly. Some of it gets to the stalls.' Arthur didn't seem very interested. And soon, quite suddenly, we were in the farm belt. You could tell it by the high wire fences which lined the road, enclosing wide areas of land which at present appeared to be largely bare earth. Sometimes the soil was being turned over by Creature-driven devices combining features of craft and of machines. Here and there were big, rambling dwellings, surrounded by open space and outbuildings. My knowledge of food-growing was confined to the little I'd learned while working in the vegetable plot at the Commune, so I couldn't make much sense of what was going on, but Arthur clearly approved.

'It's real farming here,' he observed, 'by proper farming families that know what they're doing.'

'And they're all friends and relations of Guards?'

'Most of them. Well, there's advantages on both sides, you might say. The Precinct needs food and the farmers needs protection. But ordinary Creatures work on farms as well, of course. They're the lucky ones; they eat well. Like me. I'm lucky, too, you know. I admit it. You won't hear *me* complain.'

And Arthur began to sing some tuneless Creature song which

137

jarred horribly on Person ears. Harmony and I looked at each other and grimaced, but we didn't say anything.

The farm belt seemed to go on for a long time. The road was dirt now, but dry and reasonably passable. It was growing dark when at last Arthur turned the craft aside along a track that led up to one of the clusters of farm buildings. He drew up in a courtyard and hooted repeatedly.

Several dogs barked. They were large and looked fierce; I was relieved to see that they were chained. A woman emerged from the farmhouse and called to us to come into the kitchen, which was quite like that of the Commune, but warmer and more welcoming, with a big open fire. Arthur introduced the woman as his cousin Alice. She was grey-haired, quite comely for a Creature, and friendly.

'Persons, indeed! Why, they're only a lad and lass,' she remarked, looking into our faces; and then, 'Poor dears, you're perished with cold. Come to the fire and warm yourselves a bit, and then you can get some of my good stew into you.'

Round a scrubbed wooden table sat eight or ten Creatures, coarsely but adequately clad. They had been eating and talking noisily together, but stopped as we came in and studied us with open interest.

'All right, lads, don't stare. Carry on with your meal,' Alice told them. They resumed their eating and drinking. Alice put Harmony and me side by side on a bench in front of the fire, and discussed family matters with Arthur until the Creatures rose from the table and went out. Then she transferred us to the table and put steaming bowls of the stew in front of us. I could tell at once that there was meat in it, but I had long ceased to be nauseated by this thought. It was good, appetizing food, the best we had tasted since coming outside, and neither Harmony nor I had had a proper meal all day. We ate and ate, and were given more.

After supper Arthur made his farewells; he had farther to go that night. We thanked him warmly for the ride. Not until we were seated again in front of the fire, replete and comfortable, did Alice begin to ask questions. I heard Harmony giving her a cautiously-worded account of our mission, leaving a good deal out. But I had slept poorly the previous night, and soon dozed off.

From time to time I jerked myself awake, listened to a sentence or two and put in a word myself; once Alice went to the caller and was away long enough to allow us a snatched kiss; but still I kept dropping off to sleep.

When eventually a log of wood rolled from the fire and the general scramble to replace it brought me wide awake, I saw that Alice's husband Frank, a sturdy, well-preserved man with crisply curling grey hair, had joined us and was listening with interest to all that Harmony said. Noticing that I was now fully conscious, he offered us all a drink.

'What have you had to drink since you came outside?' he asked.

'Herb tea,' I said. 'Parsnip ale.'

'Parsnip ale?' Frank made sounds of disgust. 'I'd as soon drink cat-piss. What I'm giving you now is Alice's blackcurrant wine. It's good.'

He poured generous cupfuls of the dark red liquid. It was indeed good; and, I suspected, pretty potent. I sipped mine with caution.

Frank had been a Guard at the Precinct in his day, but had retired early to take up farming. He was quick to react to any criticism of Guard behaviour.

'Don't let folk persuade you that Guards are all mean and brutal,' he exhorted us. 'They have a job to do and they do it, popular or not.'

'I've seen them pushing Creatures around,' I said. 'In fact I've been pushed around myself when they thought I was a Creature.'

'Oh, well, there's apt to be one or two like that. Authority goes to their heads, you might say. There's a bad apple in every barrel.'

'You see how we treat our Creatures here,' said Alice. 'They're well fed, well clothed, well shod. They've nothing to complain about, I can assure you. If you're in any doubt, just ask them.'

'That's right,' said Frank. 'And all we expect of them is that they do a good day's work and behave themselves.' He poured himself another cupful of blackcurrant wine.

'Mind you,' he went on, 'I don't stand any nonsense. They know who's boss around here, and it's me.'

'You don't consider all Creatures are equal, then?' Harmony asked.

For the first time, Frank looked coldly at her. 'I'd like it better,' he said, 'if you didn't talk about Creatures in such a way as to suggest the term might include *us*. So far as I'm concerned, Creatures means all those no-goods and down-and-outs in the city, that never do an honest day's work....'

'There isn't any work,' Harmony said. Frank ignored the interruption.

'... and go around thieving and fighting and living like animals.'

'And the gangs,' said Alice. 'And the raiding bands in the hills. Do you know, some of them tore down a neighbour's fence last year and killed a whole family, five people?'

'And you talk as if they was the same as us?' Frank said. 'They're no more the same as us than we're the same as you. Less, in fact. Now the ones we have on this farm are good fellows, the pick of the bunch, but they're still only common Creatures. No initiative. They know their place and we keep them in it.'

'Surely we're all human beings and all entitled to decent treatment,' Harmony said.

'Human beings? You call thieves and murderers human beings?' Frank's hand shook with indignation as he poured himself more wine.

I had the impression that he was slightly drunk.

'I might point out to both of you,' he went on, 'that it's the Guards that really run the Colony. You need us. We don't need you.'

Then he stopped short, as if he'd gone too far. When he next spoke, it was in a milder tone of voice.

'You'll be on your way in the morning, I dare say?' he inquired.

We told him we would. I felt sure he wouldn't be sorry to see us go. And now the conversation seemed to dry up. Soon afterwards Frank drained his cup, said 'Well, I got to be up early in *my* job,' and went off to bed.

'I'm afraid you've annoyed him,' Alice said. 'But don't get Frank wrong. He's a good, kind man. If any of his Creatures were in difficulty, he'd go to endless trouble for them, believe me.'

I did believe her. But it was all very confusing. Frank's strong feelings worried me. I wasn't used to coping with such feeling; didn't know what it might lead a man to; wondered if we had spoken too freely of our intentions....

'The lad's falling asleep again,' came Alice's voice. 'And it's time we were all in bed. Farm folk keep early hours. I'll see if I can find a couple of mattresses for you.'

She produced two straw-filled mattresses and a little pile of blankets.

'I'm afraid you'll have to sleep right here on the kitchen floor,' she said. 'I don't have any other space to offer you. And I'll take the lamp if you don't mind. There'll be enough light from the fire to see you into bed. Good-night. Sleep well.'

Her expression was benevolent. She didn't wait to see how we arranged the mattresses. We put them side by side and drew the blankets over both us. It was the first time in our lives that we had lain down together.

Harmony came into my arms. In the glow from the fire I could see her face. We were warm and comfortable. I had many times imagined us making love, and my instincts were now powerfully revived. And yet I was uneasy. With Melody ill, and so much else to worry about, could we really do so? The form of uneasiness I'd felt while at the Community also returned to trouble me. Was I too much a Person, would I be capable? And if we did make love, what if it led to ... childbirth? We were in no position to cope with that. My desire began to flag.

Maybe Harmony read my thoughts. 'We don't need to hurry it,' she said. 'It will be fine when the time is right. And I love you anyway, whatever happens. You don't have to prove yourself.'

'What about – the consequences?'

'Vector dear, I'm not silly. I made sure that was all right before I left the Colony. So please stop worrying. You've wanted us to be together, and now we are. And we'll get to the Summer Valley and Melody will be cured and all will be well.'

Chapter Fifteen

Half-awake in the dark, floating just below the surface of consciousness, I lay still, hearing but not registering the voice of Frank, low and urgent, in an adjoining room. I knew at the back of my drowsy mind that he was speaking on the caller. After that there was a long silence. With Harmony clasped in my arms I was sinking again into happy depths of sleep. Then I heard the bleeping by which the caller drew attention to itself, cut short by Frank's voice, anxious and urgent still. More sounds from the caller. Frank's voice again. Silence, and a return once more to sleep.

Later, another half-awakening. Grey light seeping into the kitchen; Harmony detaching herself, kissing me gently on the forehead, moving her mattress away.

Then the kitchen full of morning light and astir with life. I crawled from my makeshift bed and tidied it out of the way. Alice greeted me as warmly as before. She was ladling the thick greyish stuff known as porridge into the bowls of the farm Creatures, who gulped it down with evident enjoyment between drinking from mugs of some steaming beverage. Harmony and I ate and drank our share; it was a less palatable meal than that of the previous night, but no doubt nourishing.

Just as the labourers went out, Frank appeared. I had feared further clashes this morning, but he seemed perfectly amiable and didn't revert to the previous conversation. I wondered however if there was an air of subdued excitement in his manner; and I wondered what those conversations on the caller had been about.

'Well, now,' he said when everyone had eaten, 'we have to get you two young people to the Summer Valley. Let's have a look at the map.'

He spread one out on the kitchen table. Alice showed us where we were.

'You're three-quarters of the way through the farm belt already,' she told us.

'I'll drive you through the rest of it,' said Frank. 'After that you're on your own.'

'It looks straightforward,' I said. 'If we head north we shall come to the river before long, and then we just walk upstream. It's the same river as in the Summer Valley. I don't see how we can go wrong.'

'There's one place where you'll have to be careful,' said Frank. 'See the village, at that point where a smaller stream runs into the river? That used to be a base for raiders.'

'It was destroyed, wasn't it?' asked Alice.

'Yes. We dealt with them,' Frank said with satisfaction. 'A mixed party of Guards and farmers. *And* some of our labourers, I might add. We wiped them out a few weeks ago. Haven't been troubled since. But I'd watch out if I were you. It wouldn't be impossible for a Creature or two to be lurking around there like rats in rubble. And a good rule to bear in mind is "Never trust a Creature". If I was you, I'd take this other path you can see on the map that goes round the other side of the hill and comes back to the river higher up.'

'It looks farther,' said Harmony.

'Only two or three kilometres. And you'll have plenty of time. You'll be past the village by mid-afternoon, and an hour or so after that you'll come to Moor End. That's a hill farm, just off the road. It's that dot on the map there. Now at Moor End there's a man called Stanley, a friend of mine. Raises sheep. He'll give you a meal and a bed.'

'What, *that* miserable old fellow?' said Alice, staring. 'I've never known him give anybody anything.'

'He'll treat them all right if I ask him,' said Frank.

'I wouldn't count on that!' said Alice.

'We'll soon find out,' said Frank. 'I'll get him on the caller.' He went out, and we heard his voice from the next room. He was speaking loudly and clearly, so we could catch most of the key words: 'Young Persons ... Summer Valley ... walking ... avoid village ... meal ... stay the night.' And then, still loudly, 'Thank you, Stanley, thank you.... Very kind.... Tell them.'

'Well, wonders never cease!' remarked Alice as he came back into the kitchen, beaming.

'And then,' he said, 'if you leave Moor End early tomorrow morning, you'll reach the Summer Valley that afternoon. How does that sound?'

'Sounds fine.'

'Now, Alice, they'll be hungry long before they reach Moor End. What about making them a few sandwiches, eh? Walking gives you an appetite.'

I was astonished by Frank's friendliness this morning. Even Alice seemed slightly bemused. But a few minutes later she had given us a generous-sized lunch packet to cram into Harmony's haversack, and we were standing in the farmyard in the bright air of a clear autumn day while Frank got his personal land-craft from an outbuilding. Like the sky-craft at the Towers it was rather old and battered, but Frank was proud of it.

I still had the impression that he was excited about something and was suppressing a strong desire to talk. But in fact he said very little as he drove us through the last few kilometres of the farm belt. He put us down at the point where the high farm fences came to an end and the dirt road dwindled to a track.

'Now, don't take any risks!' he said. 'Give that village a wide berth. My compliments to old Stanley. You can have the map; it's a spare copy. And the best of luck to you!'

We thanked him, and in the old Creature gesture he shook our hands vigorously. Then he turned the craft and disappeared back down the way we'd come. We were now almost at the edge of the great plain that stretched behind us all the way back to the city and beyond. In front of us the track led straight into the foothills, beyond which were the mountains, now surprisingly close.

We set out briskly. The track was pot-holed and rutted; it had once no doubt been fit for powered craft and might still be passable with an effort, but Frank could hardly be blamed for not attempting it. In any case, I told myself firmly, he'd been kind to bring us as far as this. I didn't like or trust him, all the same.

We passed first through what looked like low-grade farmland, not worth enclosing. In a field on our left a crop of some kind had been trampled to the ground and left unharvested. On our right a herd of scrawny cows was guarded by three Creatures with sticks who glowered at us suspiciously as we went past and didn't return our greeting. After that there was only rough pasture grazed by sheep. And then the track joined the river: a broad, shallow, fairly rapid stream that flowed out of a wood towards us.

For some time we walked through woodland, with a clear, blue sky visible between golden leaves; then we were in the open again, among low, green hills with only an occasional stunted tree or clump of trees to be seen. A few sheep grazed on the slopes, and there were buildings that might well have been small, inhabited farms; but here beside the track the few scattered houses we passed appeared to be deserted. Apart from an elderly, male Creature going the opposite way in a farm cart drawn by a lean and wretched-looking horse, we saw nobody.

As the sun climbed higher in the sky, the day grew warm. I began to feel tired and a little footsore.

'Let's swim, then eat some of the food,' Harmony suggested.

We took our clothes off and swam in the river for a few minutes. The water was cold, but it felt good to be clean. In that respect I still felt Personlike. But in another I didn't. It was usual for Persons to swim naked, as they did in the Summer Valley and at home on Annulus. Most of them had no great interest in each other's bodies, though they liked their own to be smooth and unblemished. Yet now, as we dried ourselves on spare clothing taken from the haversack, I felt the yearning of body for body and knew we wanted each other in a way that, though wildly unPersonlike, was loving and good.

'You said our time would come,' I reminded Harmony.

'Yes,' she said. 'I think it has, don't you?' And, a little later, 'I *told* you it would be fine when the time was right.'

'It *was* right,' I said.

We sat on a small knoll and ate half the food, which consisted of slices of meat inserted between hunks of bread.

'For a while I even forgot about Melody,' Harmony said. 'But we absolutely *must* hurry on.' And then, as we wrapped up the remaining food and got to our feet, 'How do you feel about calling on Frank's friend?'

'Not too happy,' I said. 'I heard Frank speaking on the caller during the night.'

'So did I. I couldn't make out what he said, could you?'

'No. And I don't know why I should suppose it had anything to do with us, but somehow I can't help suspecting it. Am I being silly?'

'Perhaps so, but in that case I'm silly too. There's something about all this that doesn't feel quite right to me.'

I took her hand. I was feeling slightly apprehensive myself. What were we doing, trudging on our own through this apparently unpeopled countryside? Persons didn't *do* such things. Surely we were inviting trouble.

The valley narrowed and twisted as we climbed higher into the hills. On our left the ground became steep and stony; on our right was moorland sloping up to a horizon four or five kilometres away. Eventually the track crossed the river by means of an irregular set of stepping-stones and continued along the gentler side.

Though it was past noon, the sun was still high. We settled to a steady plod, with little to say to each other and our eyes down on the path, winding ahead as it seemed for ever. We were taken by surprise when we rounded a bend and saw ahead of us a stone bridge and a village of twenty or thirty small, grey houses huddled closely together. No smoke rose from any chimney; no Creature or animal could be seen moving.

We dropped down hastily and crouched in the cover of some bushes on the river bank.

'That has to be the village Frank told us about,' I said. 'The raiders' village.'

'It looks harmless and deserted, doesn't it?' Harmony said.

'We'd better not take that for granted. Let's have a look at the map. Yes, there's the path Frank mentioned, round the hill.'

'It's a long way round,' Harmony said.

'Still, if there *are* raiders there it could be nasty. We'd better play safe.'

'I'm thinking about saving time,' said Harmony. 'Listen. All the houses we've passed have been empty, and I have a feeling the village is empty too. Why don't we just watch it for a while?'

I agreed uneasily. We had a good view between the bushes. And as we watched the impression strengthened that there was no life there. No one appeared on the bridge or in the part of the main street that we could see; no dog barked; nothing moved. After what seemed a long time we looked at each other speculatively.

'Well?' Harmony said.

'All right, let's chance it. Off we go.'

We walked up the river bank to the village. At some time long ago it had been a pleasant place. It was grouped tightly round four features: the arched stone bridge; a single, curved street; a square surrounded by trees, some still alive and autumnally golden; and a building with a tall spike rising from its roof which stood in the midst of a burial ground.

No doubt, like the rest of the landscape, the village had fallen into decay since the bad times came. But now it was not merely decayed. It was dead; recently dead; killed.

Every window and every doorway gaped wide. In the square were the remains of an enormous bonfire; inside the houses, such of the pitiful contents as had not been burned were smashed to pieces. There were pock-marked walls, and stains that I didn't care to look at too closely. A tavern and a store of some kind had been comprehensively looted. Two pumps from which the village had got its water had been destroyed. In the burial ground was a patch of freshly dug soil, quite large: more than would be needed for one body, or two, or ten. At the head of it somebody had shoved into the ground, as if planted, a pair of crossed sticks.

The silence was total. We thought at first there was no living thing in the village at all; but as we passed the last house, a little distance from the rest, an emaciated dog emerged and came after us a little way. When we halted it stopped too, at a safe distance, and whined. Harmony opened the haversack and threw it a sandwich, which it bolted. Then, still whining, it made movements to draw her back to the open doorway. Harmony followed it, and came out again a few moments later, shaken and staggering.

'There are ... people dead in there, Vector. Dead for some time, I think. No, don't go in. You can't do anything. If you see and smell that, you'll ... Oh!' She was in my arms, retching. When

147

she'd recovered a little, she repeated, 'Don't go in, Vector. For your own sake, don't. There's no point.'

'Let's get away from here!' I said.

The dog had come out of the house and stood near us, still whining.

'Do you want any of that food?' I asked Harmony.

She shuddered and shook her head. I threw the rest of the sandwiches to the dog, which gobbled them up at great speed. I don't know what we'd have done if it had followed us, but it made no attempt to do so.

Beyond the village, it felt possible to breathe again. Foulness and death were no longer in the air; but we would not so easily get them out of our minds. I thought of Frank, telling us with pride that the raiders had been dealt with; I thought of his labourers sitting contentedly to their supper; I thought of Alice insisting that he was a good kind man; and I wondered in what strange territory of the mind the springs of evil arose.

'Do you suppose the Regent knew anything about that?' Harmony asked.

'No, of course not,' I said. 'Aria would never have allowed it.' And this time I thought of Node, saying at the guardroom weeks ago, 'You don't want to know what goes on down here, and it's better that you shouldn't.' And my speculations continued: how far was one responsible for what one ought to have known about and preferred not to?

The sun was lower in the sky now, sinking into a cloudbank; and it was beginning to get chilly. The track was rising, the hillsides growing steeper. The river bounced splashily over stones. Far ahead we could see snow-capped peaks, which we knew were way beyond the Summer Valley and along the high, remote frontier which a few scattered Guard outposts held with ease against sporadic attacks from the barbarous tribes at the other side. (Were the tribes really barbarous? I did not know.) At one point, a long perspective was briefly opened up, and I thought I saw the stretch of shining wall which sealed the mouth of the Summer Valley itself; but it was many kilometres ahead, and we could not possibly reach it tonight.

It was Harmony who first saw the hill farm, a couple of

kilometres from the path, on our right. It was of grey stone, isolated, and it blended into its background as if it were a natural part of the landscape rather than something added. She had to direct my line of sight before I could pick it out.

'Well, there it is,' I said at length. 'That has to be Moor End. Frank's friend's farm. Are we going to it or not?'

'I don't know,' said Harmony. 'What do you think?'

'I don't know either.'

'I know we're both suspicious,' Harmony said. 'But rationally, what are we suspicious *of*? Why should some hill farmer want to do us any harm? It's not as if we were carrying anything valuable.' She looked ruefully at the haversack that held all our worldly goods.

'And yet. . . .' I said.

'And yet. . . .' she agreed.

It was while we were still hesitating that we heard a sound which was familiar enough in the Colony but startling here: the low whine of an approaching sky-craft.

Craft plied frequently, of course, between the Colony and the Summer Valley, but their route was direct; there was no reason why they should follow this winding river. A shared instinct caused us both to take shelter under the overhang of a craggy outcrop. The craft was still some distance away, coming up the valley from the direction of the city. We peered out at it. It was a small, open craft like the one in which Helix had taken us to the Survey Station; it wasn't very fast, and two or three minutes passed before it was overhead. It circled slowly, then came down and landed, as I had known it would from the moment I saw it, at Moor End farm. Two tiny figures emerged and disappeared into the main farm building. We couldn't see them clearly, but even at that distance I observed a briskness of movement that suggested Guards.

'It's us they're looking for!' I said.

'But why, Vector, why?'

I was silent for a while, thinking it out. 'My guess is,' I said at length, 'that for some reason which I don't understand the Guards want to stop us making any contact with the Colony administration – the Persons, that is. They thought they could simply keep us out of the Precinct, the way they did the other night and yesterday morning. But then Frank, who's a friend of Dyne's, or so he says, told them we were on our way to the Summer Valley, and they knew we couldn't so easily be kept out of there. So they've sent this craft to head us off. Frank was playing their game – trying to drop us straight into their hands.'

'That figures, up to a point,' said Harmony thoughtfully. 'But it would make more sense if we knew *why* they should want to keep us out.'

'That's a mystery,' I admitted.

'And what part is Node playing in all this? I was always so sure he was my friend.'

'That's another mystery.'

'Meanwhile,' said Harmony with sudden passion, 'don't forget that Melody is dying!'

We watched a little longer. The two figures came out of the farm and got back in the craft. It took off again and circled once more. We crouched unmoving, fairly sure we could not be seen. Then it flew slowly away up the valley on a zigzag course.

'Still searching!' I said with a shudder.

We waited again. It was close to sunset now, and the light was fading. After some time we heard the sound again, and the craft approached down the valley with its lights on, moving more rapidly in a direct line. There was little danger that its occupants would see us now. It didn't stop at Moor End, but continued towards the city.

'Well!' I said. 'Seems we're all right for now. But they may be searching again tomorrow morning. Can we count on getting the rest of the way without being seen?'

'No,' said Harmony. 'Unless....'

'I know,' I said. 'Unless we travel overnight. And that's what we'll have to do!'

I have no clear recollection of the night's walk, except that it went on and on. At one time weariness appeared to be overcoming us; we felt we couldn't continue any longer. But by some mysterious means it was we who overcame the weariness. We passed beyond it, I suppose, and just kept on endlessly trudging. My feet, painful at one stage, ceased to hurt; or else I ceased to feel the pain.

At least the weather was dry. The moon was rarely visible and the path was sometimes hard to find, but the river was a constant guide, splashing and chuckling beside us. Much of the time I think I was walking in my sleep.

And we made it at last, just as the first faint light leaked into the sky. The sound of the river intensified into a roar; the path turned sharply right and without warning became a surfaced road, mounting to the top of a dam. Grey above us loomed the length of smooth wall which bridged the gap between the sheer mountain-sides enclosing the Summer Valley. In the middle of the wall was the main gate. It was, as I had expected, closed.

Our journey wasn't over yet. Harmony was swaying along in a state of exhaustion. I took her hand and, helping her when I could, I led her round the outside to a place beyond the wall where I knew we could scramble to the top of a rocky ridge and slide perilously down on the inside. It was one of several unofficial ways of getting in that I'd discovered when here on vacation.

Seeing the valley from the top of the ridge, as it slowly filled with the gold of morning light, I was cheered and refreshed. It was a place where I had spent happy times. The heart of it was a lake, formed here by a natural dam. Engineering had improved the dam, controlled the level of the lake, and surrounded it with smooth fertile banks. On these, lawns and native flowers had been grown, in accordance with Colonial Person taste, and elegant·holiday apartments had been built. The valley faced south-west and received a great deal of sunshine. Because it was high, the air was a little thinner than down in the plain where the city stood, and it had been decided long ago that conditioning was unnecessary; it would indeed have been impossible to control the atmosphere of so large an area.

So, unlike the Colony itself, the Summer Valley lay exhilarat-ingly open to the sky. On vacation one wore light sun-glasses but no breather; one could swim in the lake and play happily around with the sail-boats which the Colonists had adapted from age-old Creature devices. And of course the Dimension Game could take place in the open air, instead of the enclosed main lounge of the Colony. In winter the Valley was closed, with only the sub-Regent and a maintenance staff in occupation; but there were some, including our doctor, Rhombus, who liked to be there in spring or autumn when there were fewer Persons around and, it was said, the whole place was even more beautiful than in summer.

We slid down from the ridge, dislodging a flurry of tiny, loose pebbles but landing unharmed at the lake edge. All was quiet. To our right was the boat-house, and tied up beside it, their bare masts poking skywards, were a long line of sail-boats. To our left were the swimming-place, the open-air restaurant, and the paved area where outdoor social events were held: all, at this hour, deserted.

We walked across the paved area to the administrative building. It stood open; internal buildings were rarely locked, whether in the Precinct or the Summer Valley.

'Let's go to the sub-Regent's office,' I said. 'And then we're *there*, we've arrived, and nobody can head us off.'

The office of Fulcrum, the sub-Regent, was up one flight of stairs and along a short corridor. The door was open and the office empty. It was large and comfortable, containing among other things a couple of armchairs and a sofa.

Our trek was over. Exhaustion and relief overcame us both. In silent agreement we staggered over to the sofa and half-sat, half-lay together on it. We were asleep at once.

When we awoke, there were half a dozen Guards in the room, all surveying us with interest. One of them, wearing insignia of rank, was a senior Guard whom I knew slightly.

'Surd!' I said. 'What are you doing here?'

Surd looked pleased to see us. He smiled.

'Miss Harmony!' he said. 'Mr Vector!' His voice was soft. 'Well, well! Everyone was looking for you in vain yesterday, and now here you are, making things easy for us. It is my duty to arrest you, in the name of the Regent.'

He paused and added,

'Regent Dyne.'

Chapter Sixteen

'Regent Dyne!' I repeated. 'Have you gone mad, or have I!'

'I can only speak for myself,' said Surd. 'I am perfectly sane.'

'But Dyne isn't Regent, and never could be! And you can't arrest us. Guards aren't allowed to arrest Persons!'

'They haven't heard!' said one of the other Guards. He laughed.

'There have been changes since you went outside,' said Surd to me. 'I repeat, you are under arrest. I am about to report your arrival to my superiors at the Precinct. Tell me first how you got here.'

'We came from the city. We walked most of the way.'

'They walked right into it!' said the laughing Guard. He laughed again.

'Be quiet!' Surd told him; and then, to us, 'I must ask you to wait in the adjoining room.'

'In there!' ordered another Guard. He indicated the office of Fulcrum's assistant, which opened out of the room we were in. 'Get moving!'

We sat, bewildered, with a Guard in the doorway keeping an eye on us. We could hear Surd's voice on the caller in the next room, but we couldn't hear what he was saying. Soon he came in.

'Well,' he said, 'a friend of yours is on his way from the Precinct in a craft. He'll be here in about an hour, and he'll tell you what you need to know. He's instructed me to leave it to him.'

'What friend?' I asked.

'Node.'

But the name of Node was no longer reassuring. He'd turned us away from the main gate of the Precinct. Could he really be our friend?

I looked agitatedly at Harmony, who was more composed than I was.

'We're hungry,' she told Surd. 'Please bring us some food.' She spoke in the tones of calm assurance with which a Person would have addressed a Guard at any time. And, for the moment at any rate, tradition asserted itself and Surd responded.

'What would you like?' he asked; and, on being told, sent a Guard to the automat. I realized that I was indeed very hungry, and in spite of the bizarre position we were in, I ate eagerly.

'What do you make of it?' I asked Harmony in our own language when we'd finished. 'What on Earth is going on?'

'Speak Creature!' ordered the Guard in the doorway.

'I don't know,' Harmony said in Creature. 'I have fearful premonitions. But we'd better wait for Node.'

It was only a few more minutes before we heard the sound of a descending craft, which landed on the paving outside the building. Soon afterwards Node walked into the adjoining room, and we heard Surd greeting him.

'Good morning, Deputy Regent,' he said. 'I have them waiting for you next door.'

Node came in to us. He was as spruce, trim and brisk as ever, in a new uniform with new insignia. His appearance was in contrast with ours. We were still in coarse, Creature clothing, worn and torn and crudely repaired.

'Well, now,' he said, 'we meet again.'

His tone was confident and affable, but I thought there was some uncertainty in his eyes.

'Last time we met,' I said coldly, 'you pretended not to recognize us.'

'That's right,' Node said. 'You're going to thank me for that in a minute, I hope. I'm the best friend you have.'

'You!' I said, more astonished than disgusted.

'That's right. I didn't let you in, did I? Sent you away unharmed. That was the day everything happened. You know where you'd be if I'd let you in? I'll tell you. You'd be in a big trench outside the walls. Dug by Creature labour.' He added grimly, 'There was work for them that day after all.'

The laughing Guard sniggered.

'Get out, you!' said Node. He got out.

'Now, hold tight,' Node said to us. 'This is going to shake you. You two are almost the only Persons left alive on this planet. No, I'm not joking. Most of them's been shot. They was put on trial, a mass trial. Charged with usurping our territory, found guilty and executed. It was all over in no time. In case you haven't realized it, the Guards are masters now.'

Harmony sat slumped in her chair, staring at the ground. I could hardly take in the information myself.

'But *how*?' I demanded. 'It's impossible. There are three hundred Persons in the Colony.'

'*Were*,' Node corrected me. 'There's three now. Plus you two, makes five. Now listen. Dyne had been planning this for a long time. He was only waiting for the relief ship to come and go. The Guards have been running the Colony for years. Well, the other day Dyne took this to its logical conclusion. The Persons was helpless. Rounded up, sentenced and shot before they knew what was happening.'

'That's terrible. It's wicked.'

'Don't blame me!' Node said. 'Some of us thought executing them was going a bit far. But Dyne would have it, and he's the boss.'

'And now you're promoted!' I exclaimed bitterly.

'I'm Deputy Regent now. Dyne trusts me, you see. He reckons I'm capable, and he reckons I'm his friend. Well, he's right about me being capable.'

'And I suppose he's right about you being his friend! You're everybody's friend, aren't you, Node? As two-faced as they come!'

'Now, now, Mr Vector. You're suffering from shock. I can understand it. But believe me, you don't know half the story. I'm fond of you two. I don't forget old times. I've done what I can for you, and I'll do more for you yet. I've been working on Dyne already. I have a plan that'll benefit you and that he thinks will benefit him. I'm going to take you straight to see him in the Precinct now. And if you'll only be sensible, it's going to work out all right.'

'All right?' I said, my voice rising. 'Three hundred Persons murdered, and you talk about things working out all right?'

'Now it's no good shouting, Mr Vector,' said Node, tender and callous in the same breath. 'That won't bring none of them back!'

The journey that had been so slow and painful across country was brief and easy when made in reverse by craft. Actually it was not quite the same journey, as the craft took a more direct course. It seemed almost no time before the grimy outskirts of the city came into view, with the high, shining towers of the Colony beyond them. We passed over the foothills where the Survey Station was, then over the Stumps, and finally we descended towards the roof of the Central Tower.

With three other Guards present, Node showed little sign of the friendliness towards us which he'd displayed earlier on. He refused to answer any of our questions, and merely said we would be told what we needed to know when the time came. When Harmony and I began talking to each other in Person, he instructed us tersely to speak Creature. But after the craft had landed and he'd dismissed the other three, Node became confidential again.

'What I can't understand,' he said, 'is why you had to put your heads in the noose, so to speak. Why was you so keen to get back inside, after all the trouble I took to help you to get out?'

Harmony told him about Melody. Though the horror of the mass slaughter was enough to dwarf the personal tragedy, she was still deeply concerned about her sister.

'I suppose,' she said, concluding her account, 'there'll be no medical treatment available now, even if anyone would let her have it?'

'There's still medical treatment,' said Node promptly. 'Dyne's not stupid. He didn't do away with Doc Rhombus. Whether there's medical treatment for Persons is a different question.'

'We're more likely to be shot than treated, are we?'

'Well, since you ask, yes. But leave it with me. I'll do my best. And now, I'm taking you to Dyne's office. And let me give you a word of advice, young Vector. Don't you try any of this "I'm a Person, I'm superior" business with him. He don't like it. He particularly don't like it. You be respectful to Dyne. I shall march you in – that's the way we do it now – and when I tell you to stand to attention, you stand straight, with your heels together and your hands by our sides, like this.' He demonstrated the stance. 'And jump to it!'

We were kept waiting half an hour in a room near the one that had formerly been Aria's. There was a good deal of bustle about the place, in contrast to the peaceful air which had been usual. Instead of players of the Dimension Game, the main lounge was filled with Guards who appeared to be receiving instruction of some kind from a senior Guard.

Finally the signal came for us to go in.

'Quick march!' shouted Node when we were in the doorway. 'Left, right, left, right, left, right, halt! Stand to attention!'

There was no point in resisting all this. We marched in, and stood side by side in front of the desk at which we had so often seen Aria. Dyne, like Node, was immaculately turned out. His straight, black hair lay as flat across his scalp as if it had been painted; his cheeks and chin were shaved to a Personlike smoothness; his uniform was new and beautifully pressed. He tilted his chair back and smiled thinly at us.

'Well, my bedraggled young pair,' he said. 'What have *you* to say for yourselves?' His tones were those in which Persons usually spoke the Creature tongue, rather than the brisk, down-to-earth manner of a Guard. I resisted any temptation to find this affectation laughable; I well knew Dyne to be a capable and formidable Creature.

'Nothing, apparently,' said Dyne after a moment, answering his own question.

'I don't know what you expect us to say. We're in your hands,' I said.

'Address the Regent by his title!' snapped Node.

I swallowed hard and added the word 'Regent'.

'You escaped trial,' Dyne remarked, 'by the happy accident of being absent. I congratulate you on that. Especially since, as it turns out, I might have a use for you.'

'Trial!' I exclaimed. 'You call it trial!'

'That's as good a word as any. The charges were technically of usurpation. In practice the offence was uselessness. We asked ourselves what purpose the Persons were serving here, and the answer was "None". The Guards managed everything; the Persons were merely decorative. We decided we didn't need such decoration any more.'

'So you shot them in cold blood!'

'You can put it that way if you wish,' said Dyne. 'However, since you Persons have always looked on Creatures as sub-human, expendable and without any rights, I hardly think you're entitled to complain when the tables are turned.'

'But ... they'll get to hear about this on Annulus.'

'They'll hear something about it,' Dyne said. 'But what they hear about it will depend on us. We control the signal apparatus. I haven't decided yet what we shall report. Some kind of natural disaster, perhaps. The relief ship's gone, you know, and it would take a long time to get another ship here. I don't think for a moment that they'll bother. This colony isn't of any value to them. They'll be glad to be saved the trouble of supplying it.'

'And how can you manage without supplies?'

'We shall be all right,' Dyne said. 'We have good stocks of spares, and we can make most things we really need in the workshops. I assure you we've worked it all out. There aren't any problems with Annulus. I must say that if I were you I'd be worrying more about my own future than about how the new regime was going to make out.'

'Who are the other Persons still alive?' asked Harmony.

'Address the Regent by his title!' Node snapped out again. Harmony said no more.

'A fair question,' said Dyne. 'There's Rhombus, for one. As a medical man, he's valuable. Then there's old Cosine. He was in his studio with his old blow-and-scrape musical instruments when we rounded the rest of them up, and I decided to let him be. The lads can have a bit of fun with Cosine if they get bored. Besides, he was Regent years ago; we might need information from him some time. And then there's Helix.'

I was relieved by the mention of Helix.

'He walked out just before it happened,' said Dyne, 'and we haven't found him yet. I wish we had. We don't know what he's up to, but he has contacts all over the city. If he had his way, the common Creatures would run the whole system. Well, that's one mistake we're not going to make. The common Creatures are going to stay right where they are. This revolution has nothing to do with *them*.'

'What happened to the Community?' I asked.

'That group of drop-outs? We pulled them in and treated them like the rest. And I made sure we got that fellow Polly. He'd fooled around with my wife, you know. Well, he won't chase any more women now!'

A strangled sob came from Harmony. I knew how she felt. Whatever their failings, the Community members had accepted us and we had shared their food and lodging. It was dreadful to think that they too had been murdered.

'It was lucky for you that you were out when our chaps came,' Dyne added. 'Lucky for me, too, perhaps. As it turns out, I have a job for you.'

Harmony said in broken, bitter tones, 'You can save your breath. There's nothing doing.'

'Don't talk to me like that!' Dyne rapped out in his Head Guard voice, forgetting for a moment the Personlike accent.

'And stand to attention!' roared Node from the doorway.

Dyne calmed down and resumed his air of effortless control. 'My dear young lady,' he said, 'I advise you not to speak too soon. The price of non-cooperation would be a trial which I can assure you would be exceedingly short, and of which the outcome is highly predictable. The reward of cooperation however, both for you and your friend, could be very great. The common Creatures in the city, you see, are a little restless. One of my subordinates unfortunately had the – er – deceased Persons buried by Creatures in a trench outside the walls. That was not a good idea, and the subordinate in question has been. . . .'

'Disciplined,' said Node.

'Precisely. Has been disciplined. It seems that many of the Creatures, wretched as they are, have a kind of loyalty to the Persons, and particularly to the Regent, which they don't yet feel to us. They were particularly distressed when Aria's body was found among the others.'

'A pity about Aria,' said Node.

'A great pity. Aria could have saved herself and made things

159

much easier for us. As Regent she knew the code to open up the Armoury where the laser guns were. If she'd cooperated, we'd have had access to those weapons, and she could have continued as Regent. Unfortunately she not only refused to give us the code; she knew another code that we were unaware of.'

'She blew the Armoury up,' said Node.

'Hurrah!' said Harmony. 'I'm glad she had the courage!'

I expected this to infuriate Dyne even more than her previous remark. But to my surprise it didn't.

'Don't mistake foolishness for courage,' he said, 'my dear.' And Dyne's bleak, narrow face actually broke into something resembling a smile. I could see that he admired Harmony's spirit.

'It didn't make any real difference,' he said. 'It merely means we must rely on the stock of old-fashioned weapons – rifles, revolvers, sub-machine-guns – which we had the foresight to accumulate at the Survey Station. Fortunately they're quite adequate for our needs.'

He paused for a moment.

'Now listen to what I can offer you,' he went on. 'At the moment I am acting as Regent. My colleagues insisted. But I don't particularly wish to hold that post. I should be quite happy to be merely the power behind the scenes. Now I understand that you two young Persons are very fond of each other. Well, I don't see why we shouldn't have two Regents: what we call on this planet a married couple. The Creatures would love it.'

'It'd stop all that noise and shouting in the streets,' said Node. 'That's for sure. Give 'em a couple of Persons to look up to, and they'll be quite satisfied.'

'We could have a Regent Wedding,' added Dyne. 'That'll keep them happy for a while. And by the time it's over the new regime will be well established and it'll be too late for trouble.'

'And that was my idea, Dyne, wasn't it?' said Node.

'It was.'

'So you see,' said Node to us, 'I been your best friend all along, just like I said.'

I shot a sharp glance at his face and saw that it was creased into a smile that you could have called sentimental.

He believed it. He liked us. He wished us well.

King Creature, come!

I realized of course that the offer – overshadowed though it was by the mass slaughter – would give us what we had been longing for. We could be together, officially, in comfort, in an approved relationship.

'There might even be a little Regent-to-be, after a while, eh?' said Node archly. He winked.

'That'll do, Node. Let's stick to business,' said Dyne. 'Well, what about it, you two?'

'You want to buy us,' said Harmony coldly.

'Put it like that if you wish, my dear,' said Dyne. 'It's a generous offer. I ask only one thing in return. I would expect you, Vector, to make a brief speech at your inauguration, requesting loyalty to the new regime.'

'Oh, *no!*' Harmony burst out.

'If I might make a suggestion, Regent,' said Node to Dyne.

'Yes, Node?'

'Miss Harmony has a sister outside in the city, that she's been trying to get medical help for. Now, suppose she was to be cooperative, we could do something about that, couldn't we? Rhombus could see what he can do for this Person.'

'I expect so,' said Dyne; and to us, 'You help me, we'll help you. You agree to a joint Regency and we'll send Rhombus to do what he can for the young lady's sister. Simple.'

Harmony turned to me with an expression more troubled than ever.

'You must give us time to think,' I said.

'You can have until tomorrow morning. That should be enough. Seems an easy choice to me. On the one hand life together for you two, an assured position, no worries, medical help for your sister. On the other hand ... well, 292 Persons died in this Colony the other day. If that number was to go up to 294, nobody would care. Except Node, maybe. I dare say *he'd* care. But it wouldn't make any difference.'

'You're a bastard, Dyne!' said Node.

'That's right,' agreed Dyne. 'Being a bastard is what got me where I am.' And then he resumed the Personlike tones from which he'd gradually lapsed during the interview.

'My dear young people,' he said, 'I do advise you most strongly to make a sensible decision.'

Node took us to a small room which had once been used by one of Aria's assistants.

'Now listen!' he said. 'For everybody's sake, you got to say "Yes" to Dyne. No useless heroics, understand? You'd only sentence yourselves to death, and what good would that be to anyone? Talk it over and use your common sense. I'll be back. So long.'

And then we were alone together. We moved straight into each other's arms. Harmony wept. I should have felt better if I could have wept myself, but my eyes were dry.

After a while I said, 'Node's right, isn't he? We have to agree. There's no future in refusing.'

'That's one way of looking at it.'

'Harmony, we shall be getting what we always wanted. Each other.'

'And on what a basis!' Harmony said. 'Survivors of a mass murder. Symbols of respectability for a system run by brutes like Dyne!'

'Not all Guards are brutes,' I reminded her. 'You heard what Node said. Some of them didn't want it.'

'No, of course they're not all brutes. But the brutes are in charge. Can you bring yourself to prop up a regime that's built on slaughter and that Dyne admits will go on oppressing the wretched Creatures?'

I said, 'I don't see that the regime will be improved if we get ourselves killed. Whereas if we stay alive we may have chances to intervene and make things better.'

'Do we make things better if you go out on the balcony and tell people they should back the Guards? Could you do it, Vector? Could you be as dishonourable as that?'

I didn't answer, but shifted my ground.

'There's Melody to think of,' I said.

'I know.' We were silent again for some little time. Then Harmony said, 'All right, Vector. It's quite true. We haven't any option. I agree to be joint Regent with you. But you realize that this is going to poison *our* relationship? How can we ever feel right together after this?'

Chapter Seventeen

Harmony and I were well treated on our return to the Precinct, though that was no great comfort. We were allotted rooms in Tower One, where most of the senior Persons had lived; and the absence of the former occupants was both eerie and painful. Wherever we went we were accompanied: Harmony by a dour middle-aged woman Guard called Coda; myself by a young man, Cusp, who was fresh-faced and pleasant but didn't have much to say.

Our meals were taken together in a small sitting-room, and were uneasy occasions. On Dyne's orders, Harmony and I wore Person clothing, which itself imposed a degree of strangeness and formality after the weeks we had lived as Creatures. And contact between us was difficult for a more important reason. Though I still loved Harmony and thought she loved me, her prediction that our relationship would be affected was quickly coming true. She could not reconcile herself to our position as potential supporters of the new regime. It was an effort for her even to speak to me.

My recollection of the next few days is mainly of a series of episodes.

Dyne was pleased with me.

'Well done, young Vector!' he said when I'd told him of our decision to accept the joint Regency. 'You persuaded her, eh? If you go on like this you'll be quite an asset to us.'

I wasn't so pleased with myself.

'As for the speech you mentioned,' I said, 'that's another matter. I can't bring myself to do it.'

'Don't worry just yet,' Dyne advised me. 'Give yourself time to get used to the idea. Amazing what folk can get used to. And seeing you've managed to persuade your young lady on one point, I expect you can persuade yourself on another.'

I didn't know what to say to that. It seemed best to say nothing.

'We'll have a double event on the same day,' Dyne went on. 'The installation and the wedding. Appearances on the balcony and all that. And the sooner the better, I think. There's no doubt about it, the Creatures are restless. This will help them simmer down. Node, how long do we need to prepare for the ceremony?'

'Two or three weeks?' Node suggested.

'Nonsense, man. Ten days will be ample. Tell everyone concerned. Ten days from today, the new Regents will be installed.'

A few hours later I was walking across the Precinct when Harmony called my name and came running after me, leaving the woman Guard Coda panting behind. Her face was alive at last, and I guessed at once what the news was.

'Rhombus can treat her!' she cried.

'Hurrah! That's wonderful!'

'She has something called tuberculosis. It's a disease affecting her lungs, and it probably comes from living in unhealthy, overcrowded conditions. Rhombus knows all about it, he's seen it once or twice in Guard families. There's an old-fashioned drug called streptomycin that clears it up. It's an antibiotic, whatever that means.'

'And where is Melody now?'

'She's still out there at the Stumps. She won't leave Len and the child. Rhombus is furious about that; he wants her to come in here. But she's stubborn.'

'Like you,' I said; but Harmony didn't smile.

'She says if she can be cured, hundreds of Creatures should have been cured over the years, too. She almost refused treatment.'

'Anyway,' I said, 'it's a load off your mind. I can't tell you how glad I am.' And regardless of the two attendant Guards who were still keeping a close watch on us, I opened my arms and made to embrace her. But Harmony drew back.

'She's not well *yet*, you know. Not by a long way. I shall go back to her every day. Dyne and Rhombus say I can. Under guard, of course.'

'Come here,' I said. 'I love you.'

But again she drew back. 'I'm sorry. I – I don't want to. It doesn't feel right. Looking after my sister is real, and when you and I were outside together it was real, but this nightmare in here and all this bargaining over the Regency are – oh, I don't know how to say it. Unreal, artificial, horrible. And you seem to be part of it all. It's unfair, I know, Vector; you haven't any choice. But I can't help the way I feel.'

On my third and fourth days back in the Precinct I saw little of Harmony. She was away most of the day visiting her sister; and when we had meals together we had little to say to each other. I myself was not allowed outside and was accompanied by Cusp wherever I went. Though I could move around freely within the walls, time passed slowly. It was unpleasant to go into the main lounge, where the Dimension Game tables had been taken up and Guard lectures and briefings were held all day long; or into the Persons' Restaurant, now used by the senior Guards. Sometimes I would go down into the Precinct and sit on the seats where Harmony and I had made our first tentative advances to each other. Other times I would walk the walls and look out over the city which sprawled below, trying to decide exactly where the various parts of it were which we had been in.

My impression that there was restlessness both inside and outside the Precinct continued. Squads of Guards were marched around and lectured to, and firing could be heard from the range outside the walls. More than once, leaning over the parapet, I saw clusters of Creatures gathering together, making angry gestures and shouting to each other. Another time a sizeable crowd moved in towards the main gate, and stones were thrown before they were dispersed by gun-fire. On yet another occasion I saw a squad of Guards driving out into the city in land-craft, and once again shots were heard.

On the evening of the fourth day, Node joined me on the wall and I asked him about the unrest. He seemed inclined to dismiss it. 'Dyne always knew there'd be a spot of trouble when we took over,' he said. 'He don't deceive himself. Creatures don't love Guards, you know. The truth is, they had a kind of reverence for the Persons, rightly or wrongly, whereas they don't think we're any better than they are. But Dyne reckons it'll die down. They'll get used to the change, and having you and Harmony as Regents will help. They've no weapons but sticks and stones, anyway.'

'Seems they keep going on about this King Creature coming,' remarked Cusp.

'They always did,' said Node; but I thought a wary look came into his eyes. And that was the night I first heard the sound of the big drums, coming from various directions across the city and answering each other.

'I seen one of them drums,' Cusp said. 'Great big things they are. They make 'em from animal skins, stretched on a kind of round frame. You wouldn't think Creatures would know how. Amazing lot of noise they make; weird, too. Kind of exciting, isn't it? Our chaps have shot holes in a few of them already.'

The drums were sounding again the following night. But the day after that, announcers were sent round the city in land-craft to proclaim the coming installation through loud-speakers. And the following day was much quieter.

'They'll be digesting that,' said Node when he came to see me. 'Dyne has it all worked out. A pair of nice young Persons as Regents and a handful of goodies to mark the occasion will do the trick, he reckons. Most folks are peaceable, after all; they don't like trouble. Dyne's a shrewd fellow; he thinks ahead. By the way, I might as well tell you, old Cosine will carry out the ceremonies.'

'Cosine?' I hadn't seen him since our return. 'Is he cooperating?'

'Seems to be. Mind you, the poor old guy never really knows where he is, with his head full of all that old musical stuff. But Dyne thinks he's made him understand just about enough. And as a one-time Regent himself, he's just what's needed. I expect, being what he is, Dyne will have some kind of stand-by plan in case Cosine makes a mess of it. Well, there you are, young Vector. Only three days to wait now, and you'll be a happy man. Or so everyone hopes.'

On the eighth day the technician Guards were set to work. The balcony was run out from the wall, above the main gate. The lighting effects and amplifiers were installed and tested, and from the walls I saw land-craft rolling out, carrying to various points in the city the scaffolding for the great video screens on which the proceedings would be relayed. There was no sign of any attempt to interfere with the work. Creature children appeared in clusters to watch what was going on, but hardly any adults were to be seen.

On the ninth day, Harmony and I were called to the display room immediately after our morning meal.

'Here's your speech for tomorrow, sir,' said the technician Guard in charge. 'On that screen there. Learn it by heart, please. There'll be a prompter on the balcony, where the crowd can't see it, but it's always best to be word-perfect.'

I hadn't made any inquiries about my speech, having hoped absurdly that it would somehow go away.

'Who composed it?' I asked.

'Dyne.'

I felt a momentary foreboding. But in fact Dyne had been at some pains not to provoke a last-minute show-down. The speech was brief and fairly inoffensive. It referred to the tradition of Regency which Harmony and I had inherited, claimed that the installation of a pair of joint Regents was a happy innovation within the spirit of this tradition, declared our intention to serve both Colony and Creatures to the best of our ability, and predicted brighter days ahead for everybody. There was no reference to the Guards' take-over or to the recent deaths.

Harmony and I were still pondering it when Dyne himself came in. With him was Surd, who'd been brought back from the Summer Valley to organize the ceremonies. It was explained to us that this speech would be made immediately after the installation. When it was over, Harmony and I would throw out sweetmeats that the Creature children below would scramble for. We would then retire inside, and a civil ceremony conducted by Cosine would complete our pairing. There would be a banquet for the remaining Persons and leading Guards, and then Harmony and I would be shown to the Regent's quarters and left together at last.

'Then you get your reward, lad,' said Dyne.

Harmony was silent. Her face was totally closed to me. When I looked into her eyes, she stared back at me as if she were challenging a stranger. I did not believe the reward Dyne had in mind would be mine the following night. I wondered whether it ever would. I wished we were out among the Creatures, sleeping rough, eating whatever coarse food we could find, but owing nothing to Dyne or his regime.

Chapter Eighteen

The night before Installation Day I slept poorly and woke just after dawn. A little light was filtering in round the edges of the window-blinds, and showed me the dark hump on the camp-bed in the corner which was Cusp. I had no hope of sleeping again; my whole body seemed full of excitement and apprehension, and my head a great jostle of thoughts, none of them taken to any conclusion before being chased out of my mind by others equally urgent. I couldn't lie in bed, either; mind and body alike were demanding action. But there wasn't much action open to me. A walk round the walls was possible, however. Very quietly I put my feet to the ground, rose and began to dress. Quietly, quietly; but not quietly enough. There was a stirring on the other bed, and then Cusp's voice:

'Morning, sir.'

'Oh, hello.'

'Not thinking of going anywhere, was you?'

'Yes. I thought I'd take a turn round the walls. Just for a bit of exercise.'

'I'll be ready in a moment.'

'That's all right, Cusp. No need for you to come.'

'I got to come, sir. That's my orders. You're not to go anywhere without me being there.'

'Well, forget it for once. Listen, Cusp, you know I can't get away, except by jumping from the parapet and killing myself, and I promise you I won't do that. I'll be back here in half an hour without fail. You can rest a bit longer.'

'Sorry, sir. Nothing doing.'

I knew he wouldn't let me, of course. I might as well have

waited. But I was ready and he wasn't, quite. I slid the door open, slipped out and hurried over the bridgeway that linked Tower One to the walls. Cusp hurried after me, pulling on his coat as he went, and caught me up after I'd covered twenty or thirty metres.

'Don't give me a hard day!' he begged me. 'And don't make trouble for yourself. You know I've only to touch the alarm key on my tablet to turn out every Guard in the Precinct. That won't do you any good, will it?'

I accepted necessity. There was no getting away from Cusp. I strode on in silence, and while ever I did so he hung back a couple of paces in a kind of token respect for my privacy; but when I stopped to look over the parapet he stopped too and stood beside me. It was almost full light: a grey, cold day, more winter now than autumn, but dry. A little to my left was the balcony, now almost ready for the day's ceremony. You wouldn't have guessed it was a temporary excrescence which hadn't been there a couple of days ago and would be gone again tomorrow. Early as it was, there was work going on: carpets and curtains were being fitted, while technician Guards made adjustments to the electronics, and cross voices were raised as people got in each other's way. Directly below the balcony was the main gate, and out through it went armed patrols of Guards, some in land-craft and some on foot.

'What are they up to?' I asked Cusp.

'No idea, sir,' he said blankly.

'Come now, Cusp. You've forced your company on me, so try to be helpful.'

'They'll be going out into the districts, I expect,' Cusp said. 'Looking out for concentrations of Creatures, or anything that might be suspicious. Dyne don't take no chances.'

That seemed true enough. As we continued our walk round the walls, we saw Guard look-outs at every vantage point. Several sky-craft took off and could be seen circling over various parts of the city. I had the sense that Dyne's fist was clenched firmly round the Precinct. Everything was under his control.

Even with pauses to watch what was going on, it took little more than the half-hour I'd mentioned to complete the circuit. Surprisingly, I found the walk had given me an appetite. The former Persons' Restaurant was now open, and I sat at a table by myself and ate eggs and toasted bread. One or two of the senior Guards who came in were personal acquaintances, but they were either aloof or respectful, and kept away from my table. Cusp, who was not of high enough rank to sit in this restaurant, was given his food somewhere behind the scenes, but I was well aware that his eye would be on me all the time.

After breakfast I tried to speak to Harmony, but Coda, the female Guard who was watching over her as Cusp watched over me, informed me that she had nothing to say. It was impossible to tell whether this was Harmony's decision or Coda's. I passed the time somehow until mid-morning, when a rehearsal of the ceremony began.

Dyne put in a brief appearance, wearing an immaculate dark-blue uniform with ceremonial trimmings. He came over to me at once and was affable.

'Well, young man,' he said, 'how are you today? Feeling nervous?'

'A bit.'

'Don't worry. You'll be all right. Just do as Surd tells you, and say your piece as if you really meant it.'

By the time Harmony and Cosine arrived, Dyne had gone. Harmony was pale and aloof; she had no smile or greeting for me. I was seeing Cosine for the first time since the take-over, and was surprised to note how old and feeble he looked.

'Things aren't what they used to be, are they?' he remarked, with spectacular understatement. 'It's all rather confusing.' Yet I felt he was expressing no more than a conventional regret for old times. He seemed to be quite cheerful and to be looking forward to the day's events.

'You're cooperating with the new regime, then?' I asked him in Person; at which one of the senior Guards present requested me politely to speak Creature. And Cosine replied in Creature that he was being treated very well and had no complaints to make. He was continuing with his work on the old musical instruments, and had even been allowed to keep his ex-Regent's gold-edged tablet, which gave him access to all the information stored in the Colony.

I didn't see how Cosine could be unaware of the murder of our fellow-Persons, but I had the impression that he was managing, in some strange, self-defensive way, to keep it outside his consciousness. He had a clear enough recollection, however, of the installation ceremony which he had conducted for Aria when he ceased to be Regent himself. And the old Creature words came readily to his tongue as the rehearsal proceeded:

> 'I now install thee Vector and thee Harmony to rule this Colony according to Person tradition and conscience, with favour or malice towards none, and without complaint or reluctance, until such time as the burden of this duty shall be removed from you.'

And so on and so on.

I had memorized my speech, and gave it without help from the monitors, though at one point Surd exhorted me to speak with more enthusiasm. Curiously, I did in fact begin to feel as if I were identified with the proceedings and wanted them to go well and smoothly. I was alarmed to find that Harmony was expected to say a couple of sentences; I thought that any demand upon her for cooperation might lead instantly to refusal and crisis. But fortunately the brief speech prepared for her was innocuous; it merely promised that she would serve both Colony and Creatures to the best of her ability. She delivered it in flat, mechanical tones; and, wisely, Surd did not urge her to greater effort. Her whole manner remained cold and withdrawn, and she still had nothing to say to me.

After the rehearsal there was a formal luncheon. Cosine had been placed at the head of the table, and made a vague nostalgic speech about the joys of youth and the advantages of early responsibility. Twice he referred to Harmony as Sonata, using the name of a female Person who had gone back to Annulus a decade previously.

And then there was nothing to do but wait for the start of the proceedings, planned for dusk in order to enhance the lighting effects. The four remaining Persons of the Colony – Cosine, Rhombus, Harmony and I – sat in the lounge of Tower One under the eyes of our personal Guards, watching the group of monitor screens which showed various sections of the crowd now building

173

up in front of the main gate. It was a large, orderly gathering, consisting mostly of women and children; the males appeared to have stayed away. Many of the children carried flags, rattles and other traditional Creature devices for signalling approval. Uniformed Guards moved constantly through the throng, but there was nothing for them to do. And at length the daylight began to fade.

Surd put his head round the door of the lounge and signalled to us to come forward. We crossed the bridgeway to the walls and approached the entrance to the balcony. Here we were marshalled in a little line. Then two under-Guards stepped forward, strode to the front of the balcony, pulled back the thick, red curtains, and quietly withdrew as a spotlit Dyne marched forward in his ceremonial uniform.

There was a ragged cheer. Dyne raised a hand as if to quell the applause, though this was hardly necessary. Then he made a brief speech, which came back to us with blurred edges in echoes from loud-speakers all over the square. It was to the effect that a new regime had become necessary because of the corruption and ineffectiveness of the old one. There was now a great opportunity for Creature advancement, of which the Guards whom he had the privilege to lead would be in the forefront. Better times were coming than Creatures had ever known since the good days of long ago.

Yet in this new start, said Dyne, the value of tradition was not going to be neglected. The new joint Regents would once again be Persons: two handsome and talented young Persons who were in no way to blame for the failures of the old regime. He had pleasure, he concluded, in calling on Cosine, who was known and respected by all as a Person of distinction and a former Regent, to perform the ceremony of installation.

Then, acknowledging further ragged cheers, Dyne welcomed Cosine to the brightly-lit forefront of the balcony, and the two of them shook hands. Cosine made another wandering speech, which boomed and faded alternately as he spoke into the microphones or mumbled to one side. After a few minutes Surd managed to dig him discreetly in the ribs, and Cosine abandoned his remarks and called Harmony and myself before him. Node, standing just behind me, patted me on the back. And as Harmony and I stepped forward side by side the first real cheer rose from the crowd, with the children's voices high and shrill over the top of it. I put out a hand to take Harmony's. She didn't resist, but her hand lay limp and unresponding in mine.

Cosine at last rose to the occasion, straightened himself up, and in a stronger, clearer voice ordered that the emblem of Regency be brought forth. The two under-Guards who had drawn back the curtains came forward again, bearing a representation of our planet Annulus: an orb surrounded by a halo. This had, in Person philosophy, a profound significance which the Creature tongue has no way of conveying; but for the purpose of making it mean something to simple Creature minds it had been stated long ago that the orb symbolized power and the halo glory.

As Cosine raised it high, the orb shone with a golden light which was reflected cloudily in the insubstantial material of the halo. The orb now grew brighter and brighter, and the halo appeared to extend itself. This was only a lighting effect, which had been seen on similar occasions in the past, but it impressed the crowd, and an audible sigh rose up from below.

Harmony and I extended our hands forward. In a few seconds, Cosine would lower the orb and we would take and hold it between us. As he lowered it, the light would dim and the halo shrink, but when Harmony and I took it we would in turn raise it high; the light would then shine out more strongly than before and the halo would extend farther than ever. But for the moment Cosine was still holding the orb above his head as if reluctant to relinquish it; and all eyes were fixed on its hypnotic brilliance.

It was at that moment that Node's hand went up, in a movement too swift to follow. He put a pistol at Dyne's head and fired. In a split second another Guard had shot Surd. There were more shots; the balcony rang with noise. Node fell. Cosine dropped the orb, and its light went out. The darkness was full of wrestling bodies. In the confusion I grabbed Harmony's hand, and then we were off the balcony and blundering along the wall towards the bridgeway that led back to Tower One. Something was dragging us back: it was Cosine, whose hand in turn Harmony had seized and who wouldn't let go.

'This way now!' A figure detached itself from the darkened wall. Only its voice told me it was Cusp.

'Come on! Trust me! I'm on your side!'

Cusp took Cosine's other hand. As we hauled the old man over the bridgeway there were two more shots, the second of which brought a gasp of pain from Cusp. Then there were pounding feet behind us; but before they could catch up we were in the Tower. Just inside was a service climb, and a Creature stood by this, holding its door open. With his help we bundled Cosine inside, and the climb went rapidly down, amid shouts and the sound of thudding boots arriving a second too late.

At the foot of its shaft, a dozen floors down, the climb opened, and the Creature who'd been waiting for us propped its doors apart to prevent it from being recalled by the pursuers. We were in the servants' quarters, which appeared to be deserted. Just along a passageway was a changing-room in which Creature clothing hung from some of the hooks. Harmony and I quickly changed our outer garments. Cusp, whose upper arm was bleeding from a bullet wound, had to be helped out of his uniform by the other Creature, whom I guessed to be a Guard who'd already changed to plain clothes. Then we all turned to Cosine, who was standing watching us in bewilderment, and almost tore the Person garments from his back. In coarse jacket and trousers, he was transformed from the dignified personage who'd been on the balcony five minutes earlier to a pathetic-looking, broken-down old Creature; I noticed however that he had enough presence of mind to hold on to his gold-edged ex-Regent's tablet.

The Creature who had led us to the changing-room kicked our Person garments out of sight under a bench, then hurried us along the passage and up a flight of steps, at the top of which was a ground-level door into the Precinct. And there we stood astonished. The back gate into the Precinct from the Bowling Green stood wide open, and through it surged a ragged host of Creatures. Some held sticks and stones, some blazing torches, and they were shouting in uncertain unison a phrase which at first I couldn't catch.

'Mix in with them!' Cusp urged us. Next moment he and the other Creature were lost in the throng. The crowd was surging towards the main gate and guardroom and the section of wall adjoining the balcony from which we'd just escaped. Guards on the walls were firing into the crowd, but it poured forward in such numbers that they hadn't a hope of stopping it.

Harmony and I stood in the Tower doorway with Cosine between us. We couldn't mix with this crowd while the old man was with us; he was too frail and slow. But it seemed less likely now that anyone from behind would pursue us to this point. The Guards were on the defensive. A minute later we saw Creatures appearing on the walls and overwhelming the Guards up there by sheer numbers. Some of the Guards went down fighting; some jumped into the Precinct, where they would break a limb at least; some were tearing off their Guard jackets and trying as we had done to mix with the crowd. A brief battle in front of the guardroom soon ended; then we saw Creatures on the guardroom roof, several of them triumphantly waving torches.

Meanwhile Creatures were forcing their way over the bridge into the Tower we'd just left. Here, I guessed, were some of the hard core of the Guards. And Creatures were now rushing past us, pouring through the door of the Tower. As they went they still shouted; and at last I made out the words. They were calling, 'King Creature! King Creature! King Creature!'

Between ourselves and the Bowling Green gate, the crowd had now thinned out a little, and we thought we could get Cosine through. We pushed our way against the stream, still dragging the bewildered old man between us. Now I'd understood the words that were being shouted, I heard them over and over again, insistently: 'King Creature! King Creature!'

The smooth grass of the Green was invisible now; the area was being trampled by people. In the centre was a focal point: a cart flanked by Creatures with blazing torches. Half a dozen figures stood on the cart, and among them was one who dwarfed them all: a tall, broad, bearded Creature, bigger than most Persons. Ordinary Creatures were still flowing in from outside, cheering or taking up the endless chant as they passed the cart and hurried on into the Precinct.

'It's the King Creature!' I gasped incredulously to Harmony. 'The King Creature's come!'

Around the cart the chant rose loudest: 'King Creature! King Creature!' It took me another half-minute to realize who the King Creature was, standing in the glare of the torchlight.

The King Creature was Helix, a bearded Helix.

And now I knew. Helix had been born in the Colony. His father must have been a Creature. He himself was a Creature. The proof was there on his face. No Person had ever grown a beard.

Chapter Nineteen

When I managed to take my eyes off Helix, I saw that Nick and Len were among the figures on the cart. Obviously a great deal more had been going on, both in Precinct and city, than we'd ever heard about. Harmony and I, still with Cosine between us, made our way close to the cart. Nick saw us and nudged Len, and then they were helping us up. Harmony got up easily; Cosine was manhandled on to the cart with some help from below; I got on board last.

'Glad you made it,' Helix said, speaking quietly underneath the volume of noise all round. 'What happened to Node?'

'He was shot at point-blank range. He must be dead.'

A spasm of pain crossed Helix's face. 'That was the dangerous job,' he said. 'Node *would* do it.'

'So he was working with you all along!' I exclaimed.

Helix nodded.

'Yes. He covered his tracks well.'

Cosine, now he was on the cart, seemed to be getting his scattered wits together.

'It's the end of the Colony,' he said in an incredulous tone.

'The Colony ended when the Guards took over,' said Helix. 'This is the end of the Guards.' And, recalling the Guards I'd seen getting out of uniform as fast as they could, I didn't doubt it.

'It's civilization that's at an end here,' said Cosine sadly. 'Something I never thought I'd live to see. And what's going to happen to my instruments?'

Helix made no comment. He was trying to persuade his supporters that he should move forward into the Precinct itself. They didn't want him to. He was too obvious a target, they said.

Cosine had taken out his gold-edged tablet and was muttering over it, keying combination after combination. I didn't see what good could come of that. Surely there was no information to be obtained, no instruction to be given, which would be of the slightest use to him or anyone else at the present moment. I looked instead at Harmony. And at last her eyes met mine and there was warmth in her voice.

'We won't have to be Regents!' she declared. 'We'll be just ordinary, won't we, Vector? We're coming out of the nightmare at last!'

There were sounds of cheering now from within the Precinct, and the tidal flow between it and the Bowling Green began to be reversed. Creatures came streaming out through the gate towards us, waving arms, sticks or torches and shouting again in triumphant unison,

'King Creature! King Creature! King Creature!'

'Looks like it's all over!' said Nick.

'But am I stuck with that label for ever?' asked Helix.

Nick grinned. 'You'll have a job to get rid of it,' he said; and then, 'Hey, d'you see that?'

He was pointing at the indicator screen over the health centre, one of several in and around the Precinct on which information was shown from time to time; they had in fact been used weeks before to set moving the search for Harmony. There was another screen over the gate between Precinct and Bowling Green, and both of them were now flashing banks of red lights, on and off, on and off, on and off.

'The danger signal,' said Helix. 'Something must have activated it.' He didn't sound too concerned. 'It's been known to happen before.' But a few moments later the screens began to flash the message, on and off, on and off:

EMERGENCY.
WITHDRAW FROM PRECINCT AT ONCE.

This time Helix was alarmed. 'That can't be set off by accident!' he exclaimed. 'That's the evacuation signal!'

'Somebody trying to clear the Precinct?' I said. 'But who?'

'It's more than that!' Helix's voice was urgent. 'It's the final warning!'

'What do you mean, Helix!' Nick asked. 'Final warning of what?'

'It's for if the Colony was ever abandoned!' said Helix rapidly. 'It's the ultimate destruct. And only the Regent can signal it!'

'The Regent's dead,' I said dully.

'Aria's dead,' retorted Helix. 'But there's an ex-Regent alive. Cosine! Where in the name of Annulus *is* he? Tell him to cancel that programme at once! There's hundreds of people in here!'

The flashing signals had changed. They now said WITHDRAW FROM PRECINCT WITHIN 15 MINUTES. And suddenly a nightmare chorus of sirens wailed out from all over the Colony.

'Cosine! Where's Cosine?' Helix was yelling now. But Cosine had slipped down from the cart and got away unnoticed.

'Cosine! COSINE!' Everyone on the cart took up the call. But we couldn't see Cosine. Outside the torchlight that surrounded the cart, there were only pools of light here and there. Most people were milling around in the darkness or semi-darkness. It was barely possible to tell one individual from another.

'COSINE! COSINE!'

The sirens were drowning us. But they and the warning signals were having their effect. Creatures were flooding back from the Precinct now; pouring straight through the Bowling Green and out into the city.

WITHDRAW FROM PRECINCT WITHIN 12 MINUTES, said the screens.

'What's going to happen?' I asked Helix.

'You'll see, if we don't find Cosine!'

'Are we safe here?'

'Yes. We're outside the Precinct itself. But everything inside the walls will go!'

'There he is!' cried Harmony. 'There's Cosine! Going back inside!' And the light above the gate showed the old man, pushing against the flow with an energy and determination that I wouldn't have thought were in him, making his way back into the Precinct.

I jumped from the cart and struck out through the crowd towards him. But it was desperately difficult. Everyone was now making at top speed in the other direction. 'Let me through! Let me through!' I was bawling, and 'Cosine! Cosine!' but I don't believe anyone could hear a word against the wailing of the sirens. I gained distance very slowly, metre by metre. Over the gate ahead of me the screen was now flashing WITHDRAW FROM PRECINCT WITHIN 10 MINUTES. I shoved and shoved against the tide, trying to get back in. WITHDRAW FROM PRECINCT WITHIN 9 MINUTES flashed the signal, and then WITHDRAW FROM PRECINCT WITHIN 8 MINUTES.

Then suddenly I was through the gate and the throng was all behind me. The Precinct was almost empty. Across at the other side of it, by the guardroom, people were still straggling out through the broad, wide-open main gate. Half a dozen screens blinked the message on and off, on and off, all together. A few scattered figures were still emerging from doorways here and there, running for one or the other gate. Among them was a tallish, bowed Creature whom, for a moment, I mistook for Cosine. But it wasn't Cosine, it was some old crippled servant, heading for safety at a rapid hobble.

Harmony stood beside me. She'd shoved her way through as well, taking a few seconds longer. We looked all round the Precinct. Nothing. Only the screens flashing on and off, remorselessly counting down, and the nerve-shattering screams of the sirens. The door to Tower One was closed. But now as we watched it slid open and a dozen or so uniformed Guards came running out of it. The hard-core Guards, it must be, abandoning their last stand. They raced towards us.

'Get out! Get out!' yelled one of them as he sped past.

'Have you seen Cosine?' I yelled back at him. But there was no reply. He was thirty metres past me already, still running at top speed.

'There he is!' Harmony cried. And at last I saw Cosine, emerging from a patch of shadow into the pool of light surrounding that open door to the Tower.

WITHDRAW FROM PRECINCT WITHIN 3 MINUTES, the panels were flashing now.

We ran after him. Cosine was an old man, and had tired. He was stumbling along as best he could, not making much progress. We caught him just as he reached the door.

'Cancel it!' I shouted in his ear. 'Cancel it!'

He knew what I meant. But he smiled at me with a kind of triumph. 'I can't cancel it!' he said. 'I threw my tablet away. It's back there somewhere, in the dark. You might find it, if you had all night to look. Now let me go. I want to die in my workshop!'

There were running feet yet again. Helix himself.

'He's thrown it away!' I cried. 'No telling where it is!'

'Then come on!' Helix bawled. 'Do you want all of us dead as well, fool? Leave him and run!'

And as he said that, the will to live swept through my being and almost lifted my feet from the ground. Harmony and Helix had turned and were running, running. And I ran, too. The running was a kind of mad, wild pleasure. I had never in my life lived so intensely as now, almost flying across the Precinct, Harmony a pace or two ahead of me, Helix a few steps behind. The signals flashed: WITHDRAW FROM PRECINCT WITHIN 1 MINUTE. We ran, ran, ran, with agony and joy. There was no such thing as tiring, no possibility of stumbling; I seemed to go faster and faster, racing for life. The word itself beat through my brain, in time with my running steps: life, life, life.

And we were through the gate and out of the Precinct, still running. The Bowling Green was dark now, but the moon had emerged from clouds and I could see that it was almost empty. Most people had gone out through the farther gateway into the city, to be sure of safety. But a few were still at this side of the outer gate, intent on seeing what happened.

'All right!' Helix gasped. 'We're safe here!' And we threw ourselves down among them. Then I sat up and looked cautiously round.

At that moment the sirens stopped. The silence was thick and oppressive, seeming to make my ears ache. The panels over the gate and the health centre stopped flashing and were dark. We waited.

'Maybe nothing will happen,' I whispered.

'No chance of that,' Helix said.

But the silence went on. The moon disappeared behind clouds. We waited, waited. The moon came out again. We waited.

Nothing.

Still nothing.

It began quite slowly. There wasn't much noise, not nearly as much as the sirens had made. Sections of the wall first, collapsing one after another. Tremors in the earth which I could feel through my body. Then the lower buildings, one by one. Then the three lesser Towers. And, last of all, the great Centre Tower. The sound of the explosion was muffled, though the wave of air from it could be felt. The Tower broke up. The fragments of it seemed for an instant to hang in the air, as if uncertain whether to fall or not. And then with a long, soft roar it was down, and pieces of it were bouncing along, running over the ground and the other ruins and each other, coming at last to rest.

Chapter Twenty

Next morning was fine: clear and blue, with a pleasant crispness in the air. With Harmony and Nick and Len and three or four unknown Creatures, I'd slept in a fully-clothed huddle on the floor of a house close to where the Precinct had been. The warmth of bodies had provided some kind of comfort, and I was so exhausted that not even the excitement of the night's events could keep me awake for long. Now it was daytime; Nick and Len had gone out already, and after a dollop of hot if somewhat nondescript stew Harmony and I wandered along to the Bowling Green.

Dust hung in the air from the collapse of the Colony, and there were hundreds of sightseers around the rubble, but neither of us felt like joining them. From time to time a chant of 'King Creature! King Creature!' was started and continued for a while before dying away. On the heavily-trampled Bowling Green, a makeshift stage was being put together, and inquirers were being told that Helix would speak from it in a few minutes' time. A technician in torn Creature jacket but Guard trousers and boots was adapting a loud-speaker from one of the land-craft that had been touring the city yesterday. Helix had the privilege of a rough-and-ready tent, and we were allowed to go and talk to him in it. He had just finished preparing the speech he was about to make, and he looked tired and a little depressed.

'Don't you like being King Creature?' I asked.

'I haven't any option,' said Helix.

'I suppose not. You're the fulfilment of a prophecy, aren't you? The King Creature will come, they said, and here you are!'

'True,' said Helix. 'And I take it seriously. It looks as if I am the prophesied leader, whether I like it or not. Unfortunately the prophecy doesn't say how soon I can hand over.'

He smiled.

'You've seen the spectacular bit,' he said. 'That didn't take long. But how long do you think the next stage will take? Years and years, I'd say, and hard grind all the time. That's what I'll have to tell them.'

'You've quite a lot on your side, haven't you?' Harmony said. 'There's all that energy around that hadn't anywhere to go. And all the goodwill....'

'For a time,' said Helix. 'But the novelty wears off. And human nature isn't changed at a stroke. Creatures aren't perfect, any more than Persons or Guards. There are people digging among the ruins at this moment who are simply looking for loot for themselves.'

He sighed.

'I didn't want it to happen this way. I didn't want people killed or the Precinct destroyed. We've lost a lot. It's lucky that the health centre and the workshops are round the Bowling Green and not in the Precinct itself; they haven't been damaged. And I've seen Rhombus this morning with nothing worse than a few bruises. Your sister will be all right. But Node....'

'Oh, poor Node!' Harmony said.

'I'll miss him more than I can tell you,' said Helix. 'He had a hard time, working for us and keeping in with the Guards. And in the end he chose to do a job that was virtually suicide. If there's a hero of this episode, it's Node.'

'I never knew whose side he was on,' I said.

'That's how well he managed things,' said Helix. He added, thoughtfully, 'It's *us* he was devoted to, you know, rather than the cause. You two and I: we were his cause. I don't know whether that was right or wrong, but it doesn't make him less heroic.'

'And we'll never be able to thank him,' Harmony said. Then she added, brightening, 'As for you, Helix, I think that after you've had a rest you'll be full of enthusiasm again and we'll all be going places.'

'Maybe so,' said Helix, smiling again. 'And now, what about you and Vector?'

'I think we have to start again from scratch, too,' Harmony said.

'We began to love each other as Persons. Now we have to make a fresh beginning as Creatures.'

'Do you think we'll succeed?' I asked.

'I don't see why not,' said Harmony. 'In fact it might be quicker the second time round. Here's a beginning, anyway.' And for the first time since the day we arrived at the Summer Valley she stretched out her arms to me.

Helix watched with mocking affection as we embraced. 'Some people have all the luck,' he observed. 'You especially, Vector.'

And a thought struck me then that might well have occurred to me earlier. Long before I was anything more than a rather inadequate male Person who couldn't play the Dimension Game, Helix had seen what was in Harmony; he had talked to her, taught her, made her what she was. Why should I suppose that his caring for her ended there?

Yes, I was the lucky one. Not he.

The technician put his head round the tent-flap.

'Stage is ready, Helix,' he said. 'Speakers are working.'

'I'm just coming,' Helix told him. Outside, the crowd had begun chanting again: 'King Creature! King Creature!'

He stepped out of the tent. The chant stopped, and instead there were swelling cheers from the throng. Harmony and I disengaged ourselves from each other and followed him outside. Helix turned and extended a hand to each of us.

'Come with me, fellow-Creatures,' he said. 'We've a long, long way to go.'

187